Into the Vortex

BY THE SAME AUTHOR

INTO THE VORTEX

A TIM SIMPSON NOVEL

John Malcolm

St. Martin's Press ✹ New York

A THOMAS DUNNE BOOK.
An imprint of St. Martin's Press

INTO THE VORTEX. Copyright © 1996 by John Malcolm.
All rights reserved. Printed in the United States of
America. No part of this book may be used or
reproduced in any manner whatsoever without written
permission except in the case of brief quotations
embodied in critical articles or reviews. For information,
address St. Martin's Press, 175 Fifth Avenue,
New York, N.Y. 10010.

Lines from 'One Way Song' © Wyndham Lewis and the
estate of the late Mrs. G. A. Wyndham Lewis by kind
permission of the Wyndham Lewis Memorial Trust
(a registered charity)

Library of Congress Cataloging-in-Publication Data

Malcolm, John.
    Into the vortex : a Tim Simpson mystery /
John Malcolm.
        p.   cm.
    "A Thomas Dunne book."
    ISBN 0-312-15555-7
    1. Simpson, Tim (Fictitious character)—Fiction.
I. Title.
PR6063.A362I5   1997
823'.914—dc21   97-5853
                                                CIP

First published in Great Britain by Collins Crime,
an imprint of HarperCollins*Publishers*

First U.S. Edition: June 1997

10   9   8   7   6   5   4   3   2   1

Vortex: Mass of whirling fluid, esp. whirlpool; (fig.) system, pursuit, etc., viewed as swallowing up or engrossing those who approach it.

Concise Oxford Dictionary

Into the Vortex

1

I stepped out of Notting Hill Gate tube station on the north side and paused to get my bearings amongst the jostle. People scurried past impatiently; I had to move to the edge of the pavement to avoid them. It takes a moment or two to absorb the scene before I take the plunge into one of these affairs because my excursions always have overtones – or maybe it should be undertones – that carry messages to me from times long past.

I hadn't told anyone where I was going. I was alone and alert, in the way that isolation brings alertness and a sharper focus to your view of life. Anticipation buzzed about my veins. Back at the bank, routine business would be rolling along, dealers bantering and shouting at each other in sealed rooms or, elsewhere in offices, accountants and computers silently screen-facing each other down in grim statistical challenges. Over at the Tate Gallery, my wife Sue would be working quietly at her desk. Here, the damp, grey autumn was sharp with noise and shuffle, buildings and buses and people clustered about the maddened roadway like robots, stationary or mobile, in random patterns under a leaden, uncharted sky.

I sniffed the air appreciatively, like a dog that has slipped its leash and is about to head off instinctively to places its absent owners wouldn't like to visit. Hookey; it was like playing hookey. The messages said I must.

Forty years ago, over to my left, beyond the traffic lights and across the bustling dual carriageway now lined by a fifties modern terrace, stood the condemned tenement block where Wyndham Lewis, a man born on his father's yacht moored against a jetty in Novia Scotia, lived his last, blind, decrepit years. All that remains is asphalt, wind and traffic.

Someone pushed into me a little and I must have scowled as I stood my ground; Notting Hill Gate's pavements aren't for sightseers much, but I needed to think for a moment.

Paintings, novels, poems, polemic; too much reality, too many bitter truths amongst the humour. Why did a man of such talents make so many enemies?

Even the buildings seemed to be against him; an LCC demolition squad knocked down Lewis's apartments the day after his body went from Westminster Hospital to the undertakers. Lewis had made them wait until the last possible moment; his was the only little flat left untouched. Once they smashed their way into the studio they carelessly trod on or tore up his drawings, including a portrait of Ezra Pound, the friend who coined the word Vorticist to describe the painting school of which Lewis was the leader. Michael Ayrton managed to save some of the material but it was sold quickly to help Lewis's widow, Froanna, who was desperate. It didn't fetch much.

There is nothing left to look at, now.

Further down to my left was Ossington Street, a half-cocked sort of street because one side consists of the backs of houses, not fronts, where, at numbers 33 and 53, Lewis alternated two of his many addresses in Bayswater and Paddington. He finally settled over the other side of the main road, on the corner of another previous roosting place of his called Palace Gardens Terrace, where there's a grudging blue plaque on the wall. He liked to drink at the pub in the tube station, even though the area drove him to write a book of stories called *Rotting Hill*, characterizing the squalor and ruin of post-1945 England in which that randy old goat Augustus John, another long-term pal, also appears.

I decided I might as well move on.

I hadn't told anyone about my little trip but I hadn't been lying to anyone, either; just evasive enough to keep them all off my back. If I'd told them I had a distinct tickle on my Wyndham Lewis fishing line there'd have been no peace. That's the trouble with the Art Fund, or at least the trouble with the Art Fund as run by me. Because of past history, expectations get overheated. If I told them I had a possible source of an important painting, excitement and controversy would mount much too quickly. Interference would divert me. Where? they'd want to know. What is it? How much? Some would like the idea; others would hate it. Sue would want to come with me. Then when the tickle turned out to be all about nothing, as most of them do, there'd be disappointment and recriminations. We hadn't bought anything important for so long that I didn't dare to let them get worked up just then.

They wouldn't really like to believe that there might be violence, either, despite all the remarks they always make to me about past history. They never did. If they thought that violence was certain they'd have closed down the Art Fund long ago. It wasn't usual; when I tell people that I've bought most of the Fund's assets tranquilly, it is perfectly true. Only now and again do difficulties arise, but it gives them all an excuse to banter light-heartedly at me about it.

Except Sue; with Sue it isn't a matter for banter. For Sue it's dead serious. Like the others, she doesn't really believe that anything untoward can happen again, but she's never sure. I hadn't told her about this little excursion, since I hadn't yet got an actual painting in view – well, technically anyway – and was off to do some research.

Which is what I was doing right now.

I turned away to my right and sauntered briefly down Pembridge Road before strolling off down Kensington Park Road, parallel with the famous Portobello, where they used to sell antiques once, until tourism turned a genuine market into a counterfeit charade. To the west of Portobello is an area of handsome, pillar-porticoed terraces, big and confident, from an age that was big and confident enough to smother the empty rise and hippodrome of Notting Hill with such grandiose, stuccoed constructions. Even now, though the houses have long been divided into flats or cut up for lesser purposes, there's an air of leafy prosperity north of Holland Park, certainly almost to the distance Ladbroke Grove takes to reach the tube station that bears its name.

I wasn't going that far.

A lane that gapped a long, highbrow terrace led between soaring house-ends whose wall-cracks had been marked with damp-proofing like broad, snaking rivers printed on a blank grey map. Chimney buttresses relieved the flat, grained surfaces in square, stepped columns tinged with burns and provided, at their bases, weedy nooks for sweet papers to accumulate. On the left-hand side of the entrance to the lane a felt-tipped pen had written on a wrinkled card before sticking it to the wall: number 40A, basement flat, with an arrow pointing towards a gate at the end. On the other side, to my right, a square sign was neatly printed with the caption: No 42B, Garden Studio, and another arrow, pointing rather vaguely along the house-end to a yellow-black wall beyond.

I stopped for a moment, hesitant. It seemed incongruous that garden studios could exist among these barrack blocks, yet there the card was, to reassure me. Trees obscured the terrace-backs beyond, where the next parallel road formed the other side of a square of gardens fenced or walled in narrow rectangles. I crunched down the short lane, feeling almost immediately a sense of distance, of isolation from the residential road I had just left, and rang a bell set next to a smart wooden door in the wall.

The door opened very quickly and a small, shrewd face with bright blue eyes set close to a sharp brown nose peered up at me in a penetrating assessment.

'Mr Simpson?'

'Yes. Mr Brooks?'

'Indeed.' The shrewd face smiled and a thin brown hand levelled itself at me. 'Glad you could come.'

I took the hand, shook it, finding it lean and firm, and passed through the gate in response to a gesture. The man was small and wiry, neatly dressed in a dark-blue sweater, with no tie to close a khaki shirt at the protruding collar, and khaki trousers above brown suede shoes. He closed the door and I found myself in a sort of outside passage formed by a brick path and a metal pergola overgrown with a vine and what looked like an ivy of some sort; I'm not a gardener.

'Come this way, will you?'

I followed him down this short, leafy, iron-framed passage towards a white-painted door, which was evidently his front entrance, into a tiny hall. From this I passed through into a surprisingly high, light room with a big northern skylight set in the angled roof above cross-braced trusses made of slender, iron stays. The studio, obviously.

There were three more men in it.

The first was a large, fat man in a crumpled suit of darkish cloth, a soiled white shirt and greasy red tie. The semi-respectable, semi-professional effect was spoiled by a pair of creased and scuffed grey suede shoes, which protruded conspicuously from under his trouser turn-ups. His fat face was pale and dark hair straggled unkempt over his ears. As I entered, he rose from a baggy armchair, in which he had been slumped, and stood to face me expectantly.

The second man was slimmer, altogether harder and younger. Light-brown hair was cut short almost to the skull, making his blue eyes and pink ears prominent. He wore a tweed sports coat over an open check shirt and brown jeans above soft-soled leather sporting shoes. In contrast to the fat man, he looked scrubbed and fit, the sort of man you might see at a racecourse, or in a graphic designers', or talking, at the bar of a pub, about sports cars or vintage motorcycles or maybe power boats. He too stood up quickly from the cane chair in which he'd been seated.

The third man was a miserable old codger. You could tell he was a miserable old codger from just one look. He was standing up, waiting, expectant, resentful. Mid-fifties, grey, lined, almost certainly redundant from somewhere unsuccessful. A shabby grey suit, carefully pressed, shiny at the knees. A shiny tie knotted to a shirt with brown stripes. Glasses – thick – over injured, watery eyes set deep into a brow of low cunning. A man clerical, capable of enormously detailed, tedious dispute over matters of minor, but potentially disruptive, importance. He didn't smile or anything; he just looked at me.

The sharp, shrewd, Ratty-like Mr Brooks gestured at them. 'May I introduce my colleagues to you? Mr Simpson, this is' – he indicated the fat man – 'George Welling, from Towcester,

11

and this' – it was the lean one's turn – 'Harry Macdonald – and this' – the old codger – 'is Frank Smith.'

'How do you do?' I shook hands with them, getting a soft squashy job from George Welling's podgy mitt, a dry, firm clasp from Harry Macdonald and a wet, fingery clutch from the miserable Smith, who managed to look as though shaking hands either pained or embarrassed him while he did it. As I dropped his bloodless, damp paw, a woman came out from behind a door in the house-end of the studio and stood beside us, without saying anything but smiling pleasantly and expectantly at me, as though she knew me. She was a stranger, though; a plumpish, fair figure of about forty with a clear skin and deep brown eyes, rather soft and attractive and domestic.

Brooks saw her but made no attempt at an introduction. 'Please do sit down, Mr Simpson. Would you like a cup of coffee or tea, perhaps?'

'No, thank you. That's kind, but I won't.'

'Fine.' Mr Brooks shook his head at the woman and she turned away to walk silently back the way she'd come, whilst he indicated an armchair for me to sit on. The others seated themselves and he put himself opposite me, so that the five of us were in a ring. The door in the end wall closed behind the woman and we were left alone in this high, white room, which had an oatmeal carpet, modern prints on the walls and various plants in pots on pale oak tables, so that the atmosphere felt clean and green and light, like the studio of a draughtsman or photographic enthusiast of some kind.

Brooks pressed his hands together, regarding me intently as he spoke. 'I'm sure you're a busy man, so I'll come straight to the point. Thank you very much for coming. I know your Art Fund to be very distinguished in putting together a collection of modern British painting, so we thought we'd come straight to you. George here was, until a while ago, a partner in Ross and Colville, the Towcester auctioneers, and has a lifetime of experience. He's a fine art and antiques consultant and has an excellent clientele in the Midlands.'

He looked at the fat man, who nodded emphatically, and I gave what might pass for an approving nod back at him.

12

An ex-auctioneer; the appearance fitted, although I wouldn't dare say so to any of my pals in Bond Street; this man came from an altogether different end of the trade, one which sells cattle, houses, contents like silver, furniture or paintings, and broken agricultural machinery all in the same week.

'Harry has been a business colleague of us both for some time – perhaps I should mention that we are involved in design consultancy together; Harry runs our studio in Islington.'

'I see.'

Harry Macdonald didn't do any emphatic nodding. He just looked at me steadily.

Smith was equally motionless but managed to look as unimportant as Brooks's omission of any role to attribute to him implied. I waited, but none came.

'As I mentioned to you when we spoke, we believe we may have located quite an important painting by Wyndham Lewis in which you might be interested.' Brooks kept it brisk. 'As I'm sure I don't have to tell you, many of Lewis's paintings went missing in the twenties and thirties, especially some rather important ones.'

'Indeed.'

'George here has a reliable client in his area who has retained him to advise on a possible sale. The client has a number of interesting things, including a drawing by Wyndham Lewis, and George has brought it to see if you are interested and, in a manner of speaking, to establish our bona fides with you.' Brooks smiled significantly, leaving his intent eyes on mine. 'I'm sure you must be plagued by many false approaches.'

I smiled back to indicate a modest reaction and said, 'Sometimes, I'm afraid I am.'

'Well' – he waved a hand at the fat man – 'let me let George take over at this juncture. I hope we won't disappoint you.'

George Welling got up, moved ponderously behind his baggy chair and, watched closely by Brooks, Macdonald and Smith, produced a large, hardbacked portfolio of the kind you see advertising account executives' assistants lugging round

13

Covent Garden. It was held together with dark ribbons, which he untied carefully before turning to me.

'My client' – his voice was a little hoarse but he spoke without any discernible accent – 'says he has had this for a long time. An older relative acquired it some time in the thirties, at auction.'

He took a thick sheet of off-white paper of about foolscap size, slightly ragged at the edges, from the folder and handed it to me as I rose from my chair, revealing a strong Cubist sketch of a woman's head, with the face almost looking directly at you but slightly to one side, as though assessing. The hair above was shaped in a single, strong outline and looked almost solid, like a pointed turban. The sheet was signed: Wyndham Lewis.

'A study for *Praxitella*, I think it might be,' he said, still slightly hoarse.

I felt a shiver down my spine. The last time I'd seen the painting of the dark, greenish-blue, angular *Praxitella* was at the Contemporary Art Society's exhibition at the Hayward, right slap bang next to Nevinson's machine gunner, which seemed to be firing straight at the lady, as if to puncture the metallic polish of her massive, almost sculptural presence. On that day, while I was taking a sneak view, by sheer chance Sue walked in and caught me at it, watched by the stern, almost armoured mask of a face above the hands that looked like folded tubular-steel claws in the billowing lap.

There was no doubt what it was.

'At least,' he said, less certainly, while I was still staring silently at the bold, diagonal lines, 'I'm pretty sure it's a study for *Praxitella*. I really think it is.'

I looked up into his anxious face.

'Oh yes,' I said. 'That's Iris Barry, all right.'

'I'm sorry?'

Or Crump, I thought, if you want to be pedantic, because that was her real name. Her Birmingham mother told fortunes as Madame Pandora in Bognor Regis and Douglas, Isle of Man; her father was a northern brassfounder, divorced due to a dose of the clap. Iris Barry was illegitimate, like the two children she bore Lewis and they gave away. She was also a poet and writer, very poor, ordered machine guns for the Ministry of Defence, worked as a librarian, married the literary editor of the *Spectator*, divorced him, was film editor of the *Daily Mail* and became curator of the Film Library of the Museum of Modern Art in New York.

You couldn't see all that in the drawing.

You couldn't see, either, that she was as brave as hell, had a lot of lovers, married a Museum of Modern Art vice president called Abbott, divorced him and wound up living with an olive-oil smuggler called Kerroux, twenty years her junior, in Fayence, near Grasse, growing roses for perfume. She died there in 1969.

A drawing doesn't tell you that. That's all in the mind with someone like me.

'Iris Barry?' he queried.

'Yes. Iris Barry.' I kept my voice short, matter-of-fact. He didn't know and there wasn't any margin in educating him. 'She was the model for *Praxitella*.'

'Oh.' Pleasure and relief came into his voice. 'I see. So I was right.'

'Yes.'

She was quite something in film circles. Alistair Cooke knew her in New York. If a friend hadn't broken his leg and given her a ticket to the 1947 Cannes Film Festival, she wouldn't have met Kerroux. If Ezra Pound hadn't read one of her poems in 1916 she wouldn't have met Lewis.

Films and poetry; that the lives of people and orphans could depend on such ephemera seems romantic or disgraceful, depending on your point of view. Iris Barry mightn't have seen much romance in the man who, when she returned from hospital to his studio, made her wait on the steps with their newborn baby while he was having it off with Nancy Cunard inside.

Not much romance, perhaps, but she did say that he was the only man who never, ever, bored her.

'What sort of date is it?' he asked.

I shrugged. '1920 or so. Maybe 1919.'

'Oh. Would you be interested in purchasing it, then?'

'Maybe. How much?'

15

He hesitated. I gave him no expression, just a flat stare.

'Two and a half,' he said, with just a note of query in his dry voice.

'Two thousand five hundred?'

He licked his lips. 'Yes.'

'You have – please excuse me for asking – good title to it?'

'Oh, yes. My client is impeccable. I can let you have an invoice and everything.'

'OK.'

'OK?' There was a note of disbelief in the arid query.

'Sure. We'll buy it. I'll get an Art Fund cheque from the bank. I don't carry one with me.'

'Why, why great! Thank you very much.'

'On the contrary, thank *you*. We much appreciate things like this being brought to us. If I send you a cheque within the next day or so, can you arrange to deliver it?'

'You – you can take it with you now. Really. It's no problem.'

'You trust me?'

'Of course! Mr Simpson of White's Bank? Good heavens, of course.'

I looked at the simple, stark drawing and its expressionless expression which still conveyed the high cheekbones, pointed chin, full-lipped but small mouth, the depth and character of the sitter. That kind of woman, sharp, slender, intelligent and advanced for her time – very like Nancy Cunard, come to think of it – fell for Lewis readily. His dark brooding looks when young, his brilliant intellect, his challenging hostility and silences alternating with humorous, loquacious charm, like that of some latter-day Heathcliff steeped in genius, never failed to singe the exotic moths that fluttered round him.

The other three men were sitting motionless, Brooks bright and observant, Macdonald cold, almost removed, with blue unblinking eyes large in his shaven head, Smith watery-looking, as though the drawing hurt his eyes. Compared with them, fat Welling was flustered and breathless.

Holding the drawing between fingers and thumbs, I looked over the top of it at Mr Brooks, trying to stop the spine-

16

crawling bristles of excitement running up and down my back from affecting my voice. Most of Wyndham Lewis's paintings from before 1914 have disappeared. There are precious few in existence from *Praxitella*'s time. Haunting photographs of the sardonically handsome, black-cloaked, moustachioed figure, with centre parting above high brow, standing in front of unidentified paintings or the lost *Laughing Woman* only serve to whet or madden the appetite. I was hard pushed to keep my tones casual.

'I'm much obliged to you, Mr Brooks. It's a very good drawing. But what of the painting?'

Brooks's eyes sharpened brighter. 'Ah, Mr Simpson. My colleagues will testify that I never waste time. We have, through circumstances I will not bore you with, become partners in business. George has every confidence that his client, who is bashful and needs careful handling, can be persuaded to part with the work, provided we can give assurances that we have a genuine purchaser. There is a reluctance on the part of the client to go to auction because – how can I put it tactfully – public knowledge of the sale might be embarrassing.'

I frowned. That usually meant either tax avoidance or conflicting family claims. I wasn't going to prejudice the bank's purchase by getting involved in either.

'No, no, Mr Simpson. I see the doubt in your mind. Let me assure you there is nothing untoward – or illegal – in the client's reluctance. Our client is reclusive. Public knowledge of the sale of a painting for a substantial sum would, the client feels, attract unwelcome attention. Possibly from the media, possibly from neighbours and friends, possibly from undesirables. The client has no heirs or family to whom to leave the painting, otherwise it would have been left to them. The client would want a discreet sale.'

'I see.' I smiled at him. 'It is being assumed, I take it, that the painting is a valuable one?'

Crew-cut Macdonald's impassive face moved in a slight, hostile flicker and one side of Smith's face distorted in what might have been taken as the start of a stroke.

Brooks, however, just smiled back at me. 'To be honest,

yes, but – and it is a big but – we cannot assess that until we see it.'

Disappointment flooded through me. 'You mean you haven't seen it yet?'

The fat George Welling felt it was time for him to intervene. 'Mr Simpson, it may seem unusual to you, but we have had to go carefully, step by step. This client is very cautious. We were entrusted with that drawing as a sort of test. And we had to be sure that we had a really, er, blue-chip potential buyer before we took the matter further. Although I was an auctioneer for many years, I understand the reluctance to go to auction in this case. A private buyer would be hard for, er, this retiring person to locate. As it happens, I have been acquainted with the original family, through professional disposals, for many years. Since I have become an independent consultant, the client trusts me, you see. Now that we have met you we can go back and confirm that the matter can go further.'

'I see.'

I didn't see, of course. I didn't see how these four men fitted together in any way at all. I didn't see what the real background was. I didn't see why they'd come to me alone, for instance, and not spread themselves about a few of the well-known West End galleries, who would certainly have been interested. They could have conducted a bit of a Dutch auction amongst us. They would have done better by hiking the thing about.

'If I may say so, Mr Simpson' – fat George Welling gave me a sycophantic smile – 'one of the reasons I persuaded my partners to go directly to you was that most of the modern British art dealers here in town are pretty mean. I didn't have to do too much research into it; I've known of your Fund for a long time. For this kind of painting you have a reputation for fair dealing, square and above board. I asked you a fair price for that drawing and you didn't quibble. You didn't try to beat me down because you knew it was fair. I'm sure Harry and Frank and Mr Brooks are impressed, because it's exactly what I told them. We believe our client would get much better treatment from you than Cork Street or the other West End crowd, going on past experience. Especially since I believe this to be a large and important painting.'

It was as though he, too, had been reading my thoughts. Brooks was smiling at me brightly; Macdonald was still impassive; Smith looked close to extinction. But why, I thought, why not go to America, where there might be real money? Lewis was the son of a captain in the Union Army, a yachting playboy from a wealthy family who deserted Lewis and his mother for a redheaded maid in the Isle of Wight. The Americans have an interest, lots of them, from the Mellon Foundation to the Museum of Modern Art.

Or Canada; Lewis was technically a Canadian, born by the jetty and registered at Amherst, Nova Scotia. He retained Canadian nationality all his life. There's more than enough money in Toronto, where he was marooned for a while, for a good Wyndham Lewis.

Why me?

The problem was that I was hooked. After the initial joy, then the disappointment, now the renewed possibility, a thrill of excitement was pumping down my veins, affecting my thinking. *A large and important painting.* I needed to get away and be calm, to look at the situation objectively. I also needed to try and find out more about these men. Who the hell were they? What was the link between this odd assortment? Who was the woman? Brooks's wife?

'Mr Simpson.' Brooks had taken over once again. Clearly, from the way George Welling spoke of him – he was Mr Brooks, while Macdonald and Smith were just Harry and Frank – he was their spokesman and leader. 'I can confirm everything that George has just said. I am impressed. I'm sure Harry and Frank are, too. Now that we have met you and have witnessed you, er, in action, so to speak, I feel that we will be confident to continue. Let me assure you that we are acting in good faith when I say that, following your purchase of the drawing, we will certainly give you first option on the painting when we are authorized to proceed by our client. I hope that is congenial to you?'

'Er, it's very kind, I'm sure. Much appreciated.'

19

'Excellent. Excellent. The granting of first option implies no obligation on your part, either. You do not have to purchase if the painting is of no interest or too expensive for you. But I do not think it will be. I am sure we could reach an accommodation.' He stood up. 'Please take the portfolio for the moment, to protect your drawing. It can be returned when we next meet. The cheque should be sent to me here, made out to W. Brooks. We will arrange to provide a proper receipt. Are there any questions you would like to put to us?'

His stance had a finality about it that indicated our meeting was over, but I stood my ground for a moment.

'You gentlemen are partners; may I ask in what business? Forgive me, but I haven't heard of you in the art trade before.'

Brooks chuckled in a thin-faced, dry sort of way that reproached my arrogant assumption of omniscience in an art commerce whose membership fluctuates with the economic weather. 'Probably not. We have been associates in various fields for some time. As I think I mentioned, Harry and I have an interest in a design studio over in Islington. Brooks and Macdonald. We do graphic, industrial and commercial work. In the broadest possible sense. George is our representative in the Midlands, but because of his interest and experience we have extended our business range from design into interior-decoration consultancy. We have hotel chains amongst our clients, for whom we obtain a wide variety of articles, especially where period buildings are involved. Our private clients entrust us with very interesting commissions. We specialize in twentieth-century design. Frank helps us in this. There are many opportunities for talented and experienced men in this field, as I am sure you would appreciate, Mr Simpson. Many, many opportunities.'

'I see.' I still didn't, but it wasn't the time to press the point. 'Well, thank you again. I shall take good care of this drawing. And I can assure you the cheque will be sent to you immediately.'

'I'm sure, I'm sure. I will arrange to contact you as soon

20

as George has returned to the Midlands and we have further news.'

'I'll look forward to that.'

He stuck out a hand. 'For the moment, goodbye then, Mr Simpson.'

'Goodbye.'

The woman, obviously, wasn't going to reappear. I shook hands with the others and was ushered out, through the pergola and the smart gate, into the seedy lane. In no time at all I was back on the stuccoed street, portfolio under my arm, mind teeming. Somehow or other, I couldn't quite grasp what had just happened. Or was going to happen.

A large and important painting . . .

By Wyndham Lewis.

I walked steadily back the way I'd come, trying to be philosophical, trying to calm the excited anticipation at the prospect before me. After all, purchases have come to me and the Art Fund in much more bizarre circumstances than those of Mr Brooks's neat, clean studio in a back lane off Notting Hill.

2

'You can come in,' Charles Massenaux said, as I walked through his door, 'but I warn you: this is the worst day of my life.'

'What?'

'The worst day of my life. Awful.' He tamped down his smooth black locks with an habitual, nervous gesture, then waved at the air around him. 'You'll never guess what all this has finally come down to.'

'What?'

'Television.' His face twitched as he pronounced the word. 'The last resort of the respectable and the first of the fictitious. Excruciating. The really diabolical prospect is that it might develop into a sort of road show. My nerves are in tatters.' He motioned to me irritably over a heap of shiny sale catalogues. 'Well, don't just stand there, Tim: for God's sake, sit down. Help yourself to a coffee.'

Mystified, I eased myself gently on to the smoker's bow tight up against his desk. 'A road show?'

'Exactly. A road show. Or an antiques hunt. Can you imagine anything worse? Appalling. I mean, it's bad enough being forced to appear on a television programme in the first place, let alone chained to a series like Andromeda to a rock. Would you believe it? Piers Hargreaves – the very name conjures up the villain of a North-country novelette – is hellbent on getting me to prance about like a gibbering idiot on a rival to one of those dreadful BBC things. He thinks it'll be good for the business. Would you credit it?' A compelling glare came across the littered surface between us. 'The man's paranoid, you know. Psychotic at best.'

I nodded solemnly and shifted in my seat, conscious of his anxious attention to anything I might say. This was not a moment for levity. Charles Massenaux may be a smooth cove but he's an old friend, top expert on modern painting and a lot else at Christerby's, the fine-art auctioneers. I was visiting on business, well, sort of business, but so far he hadn't let me get a word in edgeways: my arrival had unleashed a torrent of dismay.

Piers Hargreaves, whose name brought such a grimace of distaste to Charles's normally suave features, was the brand-new managing director of the auction firm, appointed during my absence in France by a mysterious process of selection in which I had not been consulted. Since we at White's Bank, where I run the Art Fund, own a third share and I am a non-executive director, you can imagine how pleased I felt at my exclusion. But the City of London has its ways with such appointments, finalized by a process which defies all logical personnel selection practices. Opinions from various clandestine sources are coagulated by the chairman into a lump decision involving executive board members, share-holders, institutions and shadowy interested parties from an old-boy investor network. Democracy is not involved. As with the East India Company, patronage and nepotism are the key elements.

That Charles, as a working head of department as well as a director, albeit not a shareholding one, had not been con-sulted in any way surprised me not at all. I, however, was considerably miffed. I'd have loved to have had the chance of brandishing a blunt downward thumb.

Which is probably why I wasn't asked.

In my view, Piers Hargreaves, ex-property man and Estab-lishment yahoo, was a repellent egotist full of bullyboy phrases spouted in a declamatory, quasi-landowning bray of a voice some people mistook for a leader's. There was an obsessive, power-hungry quality about him that was blat-antly un-English. His previous appointments, commercial and institutional, had always given rise to mass staff emi-grations and controversial accounting for debatable results, yet inexplicably the man continued to rise. Well, not perhaps exactly to rise but to float at great expense somewhere near the top. Appointments, good lucrative appointments, still dropped mysteriously into his lap, not always one at a time. Amazing the way the City can behave; once a name gets bandied about it's extraordinary how realities are ignored. The Hargreaves type can survive some dreadful disasters.

'It's absolutely criminal.' Charles's face was bitter. 'Foisted on us by the City. A megalomaniac. Ought to be in Colney Hatch. Or Broadmoor, more likely.'

I nodded again silently, still catching up on Charles's TV fulminations. Me, I wouldn't have paid the new managing director in washers. As far as I was concerned, the sooner Piers Hargreaves, pinstriped suit cut for theatricals and flash bright ties knotted to offend, was out digging the roads or shovelling coal into the boiler of a hot-pie factory, the better. The man was dreadful. An absolute bastard. His knowledge of fine art, despite an abrasive spell as a trustee of the Sherringham, one of our more noted public galleries, was abysmal. He combined a reactionary taste for Victorian narrative painting with an espousal of modish designer charlatans. Yet here he was, in charge of Christerby's of Bond Street, hee-hawing about publicity and committing experts like Charles into a series of ill-defined TV programmes, presumably about the art market.

'When did he break the news?' I asked sympathetically.

'This morning. Didn't even ask. Just called me in to his office like a filing clerk and told me I was to appear on a new series about art and antiques some TV company I've never heard of – Medallion, it's called – is setting up. It's not even for a proper channel. Cable or something, but it's all been agreed, according to Hargreaves. A chum of his called Eric Waters is a director there. Phoned him to ask if we had "a chappie of yours who could chunder on about art a bit" for a popular programme they're going to launch. The idea is horrific. Hargreaves tried to appeal to my company loyalty before he put the boot in. When I objected, he made it clear that there wasn't any choice. I've already been phoned by some poof of a producer who asked me if I was genned up on boot fairs. *Boot fairs.*' For a moment Charles's normally

24

pale, saturnine features pinked into a congested flush, then his expression faded again, self-pityingly. 'It's so insulting. I've spent years, bloody years, building up some kind of a reputation. Then this clown Hargreaves, just because he's a showman whose every much-trumpeted marriage ends up with double-page scandals in the Sundays, wants to turn me into a circus. A Punch and Judy show.'

'The bowler-hat syndrome,' I murmured.

'What?'

'The bowler-hat syndrome. The bowler hat used to be the headgear of the horse-riding upper classes. Gradually it descended the scale until every clerk in Cheapside and most foundry foremen were wearing it, or a cheap version of it. Antiques have followed the same course.'

'Exactly. I hate it. Seriously, Tim, I think I'm going to resign.'

I sat up in alarm, almost spilling my coffee. Charles Massenaux's little office, perched above the auction rooms where men in brown coats handle valuable artefacts like so many parcels in a sorting office, has been a haven for me during many extenuating circumstances. His spare chair is hard, the space is minimal and the shelves of catalogues and records threaten to collapse in a bone-crushing landslide, but the welcome is always spontaneous, the coffee excellent and the imparting of knowledge generous beyond measure. To lose Charles at Bond Street would be a serious blow. My unfortunate little parallel with bowler hats might have to be turned back to advantage in pointing out that the garment is no longer popular wear: it has returned to horsemen. But you can push an analogy too far.

'Steady on,' I said. 'It's not as bad as that, surely? I mean, I've no doubt you'll do it brilliantly. And it's not a life sentence, is it?'

'Do it brilliantly?' His voice rose. 'Do you realize that this ghastly, limp-wristed producer fancies that art and antiques can be presented on the Chinese-meal principle, like a road show? A painting here, a sculpture there, a hunting Kirman underfoot, a silver jug in one hand, a barge teapot in the other. Eclectic isn't the word for it. Any suggestion of

25

knowledge, learning, dare I mention scholarship, is anathema to the bugger. It's the National Lottery approach to art and collecting. Like bingo or something. "We can do the street markets, Charles," the cheeky sod fluted at me, as though he'd got a right to use my Christian name, then' – his voice affected a campy lilt – ' "We mustn't be accused of Bond Street elitism, you know. How many boot fairs do you think we should cover?" I put the phone down. And it is a life sentence, Tim. It's a series of six with an offer for twelve more "if it hits the ratings". Well, if I have anything to do with it, any hit ratings will be on battleships. Mind you, the producer would probably like that.'

I disregarded the pun; it was feeble and deserved reproach, but allowances had to be made. Clearly, Charles was overwrought.

'What about money?' I asked. 'Any consolation there?'

'Not a penny! Hargreaves has committed me for nothing, "for the PR", as he puts it, and thinks I can perform in addition to my normal activities. He's vile, I tell you. An utter poseur. He spouts vogue computer words like CD-ROM – if that is a word – and expressions like "hacking it" just to impress, the stupid clown, as though he knew anything about PCs.' His mouth hardened. 'The pay thing is part of that "squeeze them till the pips squeak" attitude he's always had with employees. It's done to impress his usurious friends in the City who think he's clever at cost-cutting while he stings the business six figures and gives jobs to his accountants. Someone else has to pick up the pieces after he's gone. I get travel expenses on a miserly scale. But money, not likely. All for the prestige of Christerby's, this is. At the expense of my time and life.'

'Oh dear.'

'Oh dear? You haven't been listening, have you? Oh dear is not nearly strong enough.' His glare at me intensified, then abated moodily. 'Actually, I've checked what these TV and radio people might pay for outside guests like me and it's ridiculous. They think they're doing you a favour. My local garage charges me more per hour than I'd get as an expert on the media.' A thoughtful look came to his face. 'Mind you, that's probably right if you think about it. A mechanic actually does something useful for society. A TV pundit is just another entertaining buffoon.'

I chuckled, bringing a sharp frown to his brow. 'You can laugh, Tim; you're not going to make a fool of yourself in public, are you?'

I quickly straightened my face. 'Don't worry, Charles. You'll be jolly good at it. And, if it's any consolation, not many people will watch if it's cable TV. They'll all switch over to soft porn and Westerns.'

His frown stayed in place. 'In that case, what's the point? I could be doing something creative. I could be catching up on all sorts of things that need doing here.'

'Sorry, Charles.'

'I should think you are. How the hell did you let this happen?'

'Well, I, er, to be honest, no one asked me.'

'I thought not.' He leant closer towards me. 'Ask Jeremy White something for me then, will you? Ask him how the hell Piers Hargreaves landed this job? There's no sense in it. I come in one morning and the whole place is suddenly under the Hargreaves heel. I want to know how it happened.'

'Er, well –'

'Promise me! Promise me before you ask me whatever it was you came here to ask me about. Otherwise' – he gestured unmistakably – 'the door is yours.'

'Charles, Charles,' I protested reproachfully. 'This is unworthy. So unlike you.'

'I am unlike myself. Just you watch: TV will warp every good bit of me you've ever known.'

'Charles –'

He held up a hand. 'No. Not a word until you promise.'

I nodded reluctantly. 'All right. I promise. I'll ask Jeremy at our next Fund meeting.'

'Good.' He sat back a little, satisfied, and his deep-set eyes fixed themselves curiously on me as he stroked his sleek hair with another set, tamping sort of gesture. 'Now; what can I do for you?'

I put my coffee down carefully. At last, at last, we had

27

reached the purpose of my visit. 'You can talk to me about Wyndham Lewis,' I said. 'Percy Wyndham Lewis.'

He left his gaze on me for several seconds. Then the deep-set eyes flickered. His clean white hand, with long slim fingers, moved away from his head, out across his desk top to shift a piece of paper imperceptibly to the right, slightly towards him, then back again.

'My goodness, Tim,' he murmured. 'Why does violence stalk you like a shadow?'

3

I think it must have been dealing with Nevinson that steered me towards Wyndham Lewis. Or perhaps it was an exhibition of Willie Desmond's a while ago, the year before he committed suicide, with a painting that once belonged to Iris Barry in it. Although more probably the idea came from much further back than that, with a Vorticist exhibition somewhere and an admiration for anyone who could lampoon the Sitwells or treat Fry and the Bloomsburies as the greedy, self-promoting wimps they all were. Then both Roger Fry and Kenneth Clark detested Wyndham Lewis; there was always an attraction in that.

Or maybe it was just that, like Nevinson, Wyndham Lewis was disapproved of by Tonks while he was at the Slade. Tonks loathed Cubism and the Vorticists used vortices the same way Cubists used cubes. Nevinson's career was persecuted by the renowned art teacher in the same way that the Bloomsburies tried to destroy Lewis. I suppose my consciousness of his importance could have started with *Praxitella*'s neighbour at the Hayward, Nevinson and his machine gunner in *La Mitrailleuse*, although Lewis sharply disassociated himself from Nevinson's Futurist polemic. He said that he owed his equanimity under heavy shelling in Flanders to having been battle-trained by hearing Marinetti imitating the same explosions on the lecture platform, with Nevinson in support on a drum.

Quite recently I bought a Nevinson for the Art Fund under extreme circumstances, involving fire, murder, hate and old, long-lost war scores being paid off among the filled, tranquil trenches of Lens, Loos and Passchendaele. Wyndham Lewis was a battery officer at Passchendaele and survived both bombardment and crawling out to exposed observation posts under fire. Heavy artillery fascinated him then, but the experience changed his perception of abstraction and mechanisms; he moved to more representational stuff after that.

So perhaps it was quite simply some echoes from the First World War which still, despite the long-gone years, broods about the country with its unwanted existence and effects like a debilitating virus, ME or something like that, half-exhausting, half-infuriating. Someone said recently that just about everyone who took part in that war is dead now, but it still has the power to unnerve us at regular intervals.

It might have been a memory-image from the Imperial War Museum though, *A Battery Shelled* or one of those, or that pink, naked woman's back, live flesh, amongst a rattling collection of piled corpse-bones and grinning grey skulls, horrid effect, that had stuck at the back of my brain. Strong meat, those Vorticist images; not the safe, soft, unchallenging landscapes of England's acceptable painters. Not like the placid Impressionists either; hard metallic outlines don't mix with the rippling meadows of the Seine.

'Me?' I said. 'Me? Violence? Stalk? Shadows? I can't think what you can possibly mean, Charles.'

He grinned sardonically. 'Oh yes, you can. You know damned well what I mean. And if you're picking on Wyndham Lewis, you're picking on a dead certainty for trouble. Deep trouble.'

'What makes you say that?'

He rolled his eyes at me. 'Don't act the innocent, Tim. Not with me. You can act the innocent with lots of people, but not me. Wyndham Lewis? An alien force from another planet, with an inner rage?'

'Eh? An alien force? Oh, I get it – you're quoting someone. Who?'

'Julian Symons. And Julian Symons, you may remember, was a crime novelist as well as a man of letters. He knew Lewis quite well; Lewis was a friend of his brother A.J.'s.'

'Ah.'

'You're very cryptic today. Ah, indeed; is that all you can say?'

'Why do you think that if I pick on Lewis, trouble is a dead certainty?'

'Because it is. Anything connected with him is bound to lead to trouble. You are, after all, speaking of the man who Symons said was, in the thirties, without doubt the most hated writer in England.'

'Did he?'

'Yes, he did. That is one of the problems with Wyndham Lewis. I mean that he wrote brilliantly as well as painted. People here hate versatility; it mucks up all those neat mental pigeonholes that help to avoid that thinking feeling.' Charles's severe expression changed for just a moment to one of grudging admiration. 'I have to admit that he was a fantastic painter. Bloody marvellous. His drawing knocks everyone else into a cocked hat. The Slade crowd – Augustus John, Orpen, McEvoy, Nevinson, all of them – were no slouches when it came to drawing. But Lewis; my God, he could draw.'

'And paint?'

Charles puffed out his lips, then retracted them. 'He is one of the most important British artists of the twentieth century.'

I sat still for a moment. There are times when, in looking for works to add to the Art Fund, a sensation comes over me, a sensation hard to describe, which makes prickles go down my spine and involuntary mini-shivers congeal the flesh on my back. There is a feeling of momentary void, of a timeless pause that freezes the relentless clock for a few fleeting seconds. It doesn't happen often but I felt it now: this is it, the sensation said, this is one you have to pursue, it was meant to happen. From now on the sequence of events is inevitable.

Funny that it should start with those four men, though; how the hell did they fit together?

'I say, Tim, are you all right?'

Charles's voice cut into my void.

'Sorry?' I murmured. 'Something wrong?'

31

'You've gone all rummy-looking. Bit pale. Someone walk over your grave?'

'I, er, I was just distracted. Thoughts went off at a tangent. For you to say that about an artist is unusual, Charles. Praise indeed.'

'Didn't say I liked him, did I? Just that he is important. Way ahead of the pack. Understood that Impressionism was passé – over and done with – while half the celebrities here were still practising it. Had a grip on Cubism and Abstraction, too. No wonder they thought he'd dropped in from Mars. He never mellowed in any way.' Charles screwed his eyes closed for a moment in thought, then said, 'There's something someone wrote about him being like a raw mechanism in a field, spiky and heavily plated, as though he'd dropped in from another planet. A hostile planet, of course. Lewis saw himself as a natural enemy; something from outer space.'

'Mars was right, actually. It was Rothenstein's view of him.'

'Ten marks to Timmy. I remember now. Sir John himself.'

'*Modern English Painters*?'

'Precisely.'

'Although he was half-American, wasn't he? Wyndham Lewis, I mean.'

'Indeed he was. You have been doing some homework. When you do homework on an artist like Lewis I reach for my bulletproof vest. The very name is synonymous with machine guns. What do you want to know?'

I ignored his implications and gestured at the shelf close to me, where the *Art Sales Index* weighted the sagging woodwork with its ranks of chunkily volumed statistics.

'There's not a lot to go on,' I said. 'Not recently, anyway.'

A sly smile came to Charles's lips. He glanced at the *Index* and shook his head slowly. 'Books,' he murmured, 'can only tell us a limited amount. For real information we need people.'

'Agreed. That is why I am here.'

'I am encouraged to think that the failure of recorded auction price records has convinced you of my humble value to this establishment. Quite apart from drawing your rare, estimable self to these distant premises so soon after your return from the land of the frog-eaters.'

I grinned at him. I had been away in France carrying out an assignment in conjunction with White's correspondent bank in Paris, Maucourt Frères, under the auspices of Sir Richard White, an ex-chairman who has semi-retired to the Dordogne, but still keeps an active oar in both Paris and London establishments.

'Pompous bugger you are, Charles. You know you're indispensable.'

'I hope that, when the moment arrives, you will convince Piers Hargreaves of that.'

'The moment will not arrive. Or rather, if such an arrival were to be suggested, Hargreaves would be thrown out of his office window without my raising the sash.'

He beamed at me broadly. 'Dear Tim. Still a lad at heart. Would that it could be so. But alas, the energetic reactions of your rugby-playing youth are no longer considered correct behaviour. We are mature men now, in responsible positions. When I was up at college, men like Hargreaves were thrown into the river at regular intervals until they learned to moderate their attitudes and ceased to show off. Such corrections are absent from society now.'

'Unfortunately.'

'Perhaps. But I am still, as ever, flattered that you of all people come to consult me. You are quite right; no major work by Wyndham Lewis has set any value standard lately. Drawings and so forth appear regularly at auction.' He gestured dismissively. 'They sell for a few thousand each. There have been a couple of minor oil portraits in the last ten years; they fetched thirty thousand or so. He is, after all, one of the finest portraitists ever. But an important painting, no. It is not surprising in some ways. Most of the known works of any significance are in public galleries, quite a few in private collections. But notable ones are missing. Especially a huge one like *Kermesse*, for instance.' His long face moved closer to mine. 'Don't tell me you've located one?'

'Er, no, Charles, I haven't. But I've had a sort of premonition about Wyndham Lewis. The Art Fund ought to have one. A good one, I mean.'

He shook his head sadly. 'When I hear those words I quake. On previous occasions, your premonitions have led to awful consequences.'

'That is a total misrepresentation, Charles. Every single event was entirely coincidental, explicable, and not my responsibility.'

'Oh yeah?'

'I shall ignore your scepticism and ask you to keep to your professional opinion rather than uttering characteristically cynical expressions. I would like to know what you think a major Lewis painting would fetch now, in the current, rather depressed art market?'

His features arranged themselves into immobility. His eyes rested unblinkingly upon me. A few seconds passed. Then –

'Tim,' he queried, 'does your dear wife know what you're up to?'

4

'I am going,' she said, standing on the rug in front of the fireplace and looking down at me where I sat on the big settee, 'to Glasgow. For several days.'

I looked back up into my wife's large blue eyes, raised my brows in what I hoped was the civilized querying expression of the modern, rational, understanding husband, and questioned, mildly: 'Glasgow?'

'The Burrell Collection and others have convened a workshop for curators which I have been asked to attend at short notice because James has been taken ill.'

'Ah,' I said. And then, 'I see. Well, that should be very interesting for you, Sue.'

A slightly puzzled expression flitted across her forehead, causing her full brown brows to twitch. Behind her, my large marine oil painting by Clarkson Stanfield, of hulks on the Medway, imposed a sort of sepia backwash to the delightful spectacle Sue presents when the reaction from me is not what she expects. Sue is a curator at the Tate Gallery, where she spends her days in the mysterious administration of exhibitions from an office deep in the bulkheaded basement, like the engine-room officer of an enormous liner whose distant propulsion machinery throbs away in a remote, sound-proofed choir.

She is also, as it happens, an expert on French Impressionism, quite apart from having a formal knowledge of art culled from the Courtauld and elsewhere which far exceeds my own, crass, commercial interest in the investment aspects of the subject. Indeed, she finds me distressingly barbarian when it comes to the finer points of her all-absorbing vocation. On the other hand, for some reason she and Charles Massenaux are great mutual admirers, even though it can be argued that he, as an auctioneer, is at the extreme cutting edge of crass commercialism. Hence his query to me earlier this afternoon.

'I had hoped,' she said, with perhaps more than a nuance of disapproval in her voice, 'that you might express polite, if not genuine, regret at my enforced absence.'

I sprang to my feet and swept my arms round her in an exaggerated gesture. 'My dear Sue! I shall miss you terribly. You know I always do. I am sure the decision to go was not made lightly. But I didn't want to cause you any upset or, dare I say it, guilt, at the way your work is bound to come between us from time to time. Mine does, as with my recent absence, and you accept the fact with stoic equanimity.' I planted a cautious, chaste kiss on her cheek. 'It would be churlish, chauvinistic, worse, possibly even *incorrect* for me to show displeasure, let alone go into a childish male tantrum, just because you have your own – what should I call it? – *agenda* to observe. Would it not?'

She swayed slightly back from my embrace and looked at me from under lowered lids. 'Stop the mock-PC, you pompous idiot. What are you up to?'

'Me? Up to? What can you mean? What are you suggesting?'

'I mean,' she said, disengaging fully and looking intently up into my face, 'that I can always sense when you are concealing something from me. Normally, when I say that I am going to be away, you react with disgruntled irascibility. Bugger it, Sue, you say, and then demand how some aspect of your personal wellbeing or comfort is going to be affected. In a way it is reassuring. A girl likes to feel that, however badly expressed, her beloved feels dismay at her departure.'

'You're very difficult this evening. If I grumble it's wrong. If I accept resignedly it's ditto. I am confused.'

'Not you. What are you planning?'

'Me? Planning? Nothing.'

'Liar.'

She grinned at me suddenly and stepped back to the

mantelpiece to pick up her glass of sherry. Around us, the living room of our flat in Onslow Gardens waited expectantly for my reaction to the accusation. The long windows overlooking the Gardens were half-curtained against the gathering evening gloom but the aspect inside was cheerful enough. To counterbalance my big romantic, vulgar marine painting, as Sue thinks of it whilst tolerating its presence, were her paintings: a Sylvia Gosse still life, a circus of Laura Knight's, a wistful child by Dod Procter, an urchin of Elizabeth Stanhope Forbes's and an interior by Ethel Walker. This emphasis on lady artists says a lot about Sue, just as, I suppose, my RAF Seago, Augustus John etching of Dorelia, watercolour of Bosham by Wilson Steer, putteed soldier by Orpen – the First World War again – say things about me.

Then, perhaps, her watercolour of a suburban angel sitting in a garden full of washing, by Stanley Spencer, might say things about both of us, eventually.

'Sue! Would I lie to you?'

'Without the slightest hesitation.'

'Sue!'

'Oh, not about anything really important. Important, that is, by your definition of importance.'

'I am devastated. I had no idea that you had such a cynical view of me.'

'I am not a cynic.'

'A cynic is one who distrusts the motives of others. By that definition you are behaving cynically.'

She ignored that because it was too accurate and put her head on one side. 'Let me think. I don't believe it's another woman.'

'There has never been another woman.'

'Not since we married, perhaps. But a wife cannot ignore such possibilities. I think, however, I would know if that were the danger.'

'Really, Sue. This is too clinical.'

'Ah.' Her expression clarified. 'Of course. What acquisitions are you currently making for the Art Fund?'

I blinked at her. 'None at all.'

'None?'

'No, none. Indeed, we have a meeting tomorrow to discuss policy because we have been lying fallow for a while, especially in view of the depressed state of things. Galleries have gone out of business in the last few years. The others are hanging on for dear life, hoping that every purchasing swallow heralds a ripe summer harvest. It is very patchy just now. The trustees have no work in prospect.'

'But you are thinking of making an acquisition, aren't you? Despite what Jeremy and Geoffrey might say? You're incapable of leaving things for too long, you and Jeremy. The real question will be what to buy. On that you may well differ.'

'Oh, I don't know, Jeremy and I –'

'Do not always see eye to eye even though mostly you can agree. But that's not the reason you don't want me to know about it.'

'Sue! My life is an open book to you.'

'No, it isn't. Let me think: which artist might you be looking at of whose acquisition I might disapprove?' She put on a thoughtful look. 'Someone, presumably not currently in vogue or selling at a premium whose work you vultures think you might pick up for a reasonable sum?'

It's a bit unnerving, this sort of thing. I mean, I suppose you could point out that it is hardly very difficult for Sue to go into an accurate analytical mode, but a bloke does like to have something of his life that isn't so bloody evident. I thought briefly about the reply Charles had given after his question concerning Sue.

'Wyndham Lewis,' he had drawled slowly. 'An important Wyndham Lewis? Very difficult to say what the price would be. Fifty to a hundred thousand, perhaps.'

'Is that all? That'd be bloody cheap.'

He retracted quickly in qualification of his remark. 'Well, it depends, of course. Things are very down today. I don't think Lewis has broken any important barriers yet, you see. Although you could be right; there was an Edward Wadsworth went for a hundred and sixty thousand not long ago. He's one of the Vorticists. More limited than Lewis, of course, who he funded for a while.'

'Not as important, either, much as I like him.'

'Mmm. But there has to be a progression, you know, to give people confidence. If a Lewis is to go over, say two hundred thousand, there'd have to be a build-up.'

'I should have thought that American galleries and our own would jump at an important Wyndham Lewis. They are rare. Massive funds might be available.'

Charles pursed his lips. 'He's not exactly under-represented in public galleries. The Imperial War Museum. Edinburgh. Manchester. Several provincial galleries, in fact. The Tate, of course' – he rolled his eyes significantly at me in acknowledgement of my wife's invisible presence at that celebrated collection – 'has *Planners*, *Bagdad*, and two of the most famous: the *Portrait of Edith Sitwell* and *The Crowd*. Not to mention the abstract *Workshop* and that late 1945 thing – the one they never put on the wall – *A Canadian War Factory*, that's it. It's not as though they'll rush to buy another Lewis. No, I think you've picked the right moment, Tim.' He smiled at me flatteringly. 'As you so often have before. With some rather disturbing side effects.'

'Thank you,' I had replied, with a laudable degree of restraint. All this harping on the violent events of the past may amuse people like Charles, but it's a veritable minefield in my relationship with Sue. There have been occasions when the marriage has gone on to very thin ice over my activities in that direction. She has come to accept that I do not in any way go out to encourage mayhem and that my assurances to her in that regard are entirely sincere but – and it is a big but – she doesn't like the prospect. Not at all. Why it happens is inexplicable, but it happens. So she naturally takes a close interest.

'Come on,' she now said, still concentrating. 'Don't look so impenetrable. Give me a clue.'

'Sue, really, there is no –'

'Tim!'

'Oh, all right. A clue. Let me think. Blast.'

'There's no need – what did you say?'

'Blast. That's a giveaway: blast. And bombardier?'

'Oh, no. Not the Vorticists' manifesto, Tim?'

'Have another sherry.'

She put her hands to her face. 'Oh, Tim. Not – it must be – Wyndham Lewis?'

'Here. I've topped up your glass.'

'Tim, Tim, *Tim*. Wyndham Lewis? A marvellous choice, for once. But I think I'll cancel my trip to Glasgow.'

'No, no. You mustn't do that.'

'Why not?'

'Because there is no reason. I have merely started to think along these lines. Just a first concept, not a *fait accompli*. I've chatted to Charles and – '

'Charles? You've been to see Charles? In Bond Street?'

'Well, yes, but – '

'Oh, my God. That means you're off already. Where is it?'

'Where is what?'

'The Wyndham Lewis painting you have in view.'

'Sue, you are not listening to me. It is merely a concept at this stage. I don't think I'm going to tell Jeremy just yet because he's not much attracted to Cubism and Abstraction, let alone Vorticism. I merely wanted, first, to air the idea with Charles and, of course, you, before I – '

'You liar! You rotten liar! You weren't going to tell me at all!'

'Of course I was. You've been so abstracted – if you'll pardon the pun – by your imminent departure for Glasgow that I haven't had a chance to mention it since I got home.'

I managed to look her straight in the eye as I said this. She held my gaze for several seconds, poor girl, while her sense of fair play took in the excuse. Then, slowly, she took a sip of sherry from her glass. Her eyes narrowed a little.

'There's no need to look so suspicious, Sue.'

'I don't trust you.'

'Why not? Why on earth not? What possible harm can there be in my considering one of the major artists of the twentieth century, currently rather neglected, as a potential acquisition for the Art Fund?'

'Because there isn't one coming up at auction, or you'd have said. That means you've got some clandestine source in view. Or a hunt of some kind, like a paper chase with fatal embellishments.'

'Sue! Really! This is extreme. Almost surreal. I can't believe I'm hearing this.'

'In life – as you so often say – you take as you find. Well, I know how I find you.'

'Guilty as charged?'

'Absolutely.'

I went to the nearby sideboard and poured myself another medium-to-large whisky. I sighed loudly. I cast my eye over the large bookcase that runs all along the inner wall and reflected that we hadn't got anything much on Wyndham Lewis and I'd have to rectify that. I put some water in the whisky and sighed loudly again before I took a gulp from the tumbler and turned to face her.

'I have decided to take up smoking,' I announced.

'*What?*'

'Smoking. One has to think of the future, after all. They say it prevents Alzheimer's disease. Senile dementia, you know. If you smoke, at least your mind remains fully active until you die an appalling death. It may take time to get the taste again, as it certainly did at prep school, but there'll be plenty of that to spare. The empty brain will be kept in full working order whilst, uneventfully, the long years wind by.'

'Oh, stop it. Just stop it. Don't be ridiculous, Tim.'

'I mean, nothing is going to happen while you go away to Glasgow for a few days. What could possibly happen? How many days is it, by the way?'

'It would have been four,' she said. 'Possibly five.'

'Well, there you are. What could possibly happen in four days while I start to do a bit of research?'

'Research?'

'Yes. Reading, that sort of thing. I've never read much of Lewis's stuff. There are the novels; *Tarr*, for instance. An early rape drama. Then a mass of polemical writing. It'll take an age to get through that.' I looked at the bookcase again. 'We haven't got a copy of Walter Michel's book with all the work illustrated in it, have we?'

'You know jolly well we haven't.'

'Oh. Well, perhaps if I just slipped along to the Imperial War Museum and then the Tate, to take a gander at –'

I stopped. Her face was within an inch of mine.

'You,' she said through clenched teeth, 'are not going to the Imperial War Museum without me. And if you go so much as within half a mile of the Tate without my being there, I'll – I'll – it will be the end. *The end*. Do you hear me?'

'I hear you, Sue.'

'You promise you'll go near neither place until I get back?'

'I promise.'

'Cross your heart?'

I grinned at her. 'Cross my heart and hope to die. I shall avoid the Imperial War Museum and the Tate Gallery until you return, Sue. As the Duke of Wellington used to say, you may depend upon it.'

'Oh, God.'

'What?'

'Here you go again, I suppose?'

'Perhaps,' I said. 'Perhaps, no more.' I looked back to the bookcase, thinking of the titles I needed. 'For the moment, I think I may postpone my order for cigarettes.'

5

The first of the garden-studio gang to go was the miserable old codger, Smith. Apparently it happened the day after our meeting.

The first I knew of it was when I went into the office a day or two after Sue's departure for Glasgow and was met by Penny, my secretary, a girl I have to share with a pedantic beggar who calculates actuarial risks and such for insurance purposes and other euphemistically defined activities which, outside merchant banking, are defined by the verb 'to gamble'.

Normally Penny does not meet me on arrival, having her own little snug she shares with my boss Jeremy White's secretary, but this time, as I was opening my door, she bounded up with a note in her hand and an expression that said I was late. Pinned to the note was a newspaper cutting.

The note was from Brooks. In rather precise, black felt-tip writing, fine line, perhaps slightly shaky, it said: *Due to the tragic death of our colleague, Frank Smith, we regret we will be a little delayed. Please be assured, however, that this sad event will not prevent our continuing with our agreement. I will be in touch shortly.*

The signature was clear but there was no address on the note. Nor was there any telephone number. I half-muttered something to myself; I'd sent the cheque for the Iris Barry drawing off the day before. The portrait itself was in the drawer of an architect's chest behind my desk.

'Someone you knew?' asked Penny, sympathy and curiosity blending in unequal measure in her tones; the curiosity had by far the upper hand.

The cutting was from a Leicester evening newspaper. It said that a man by the name of Frank Smith, aged fifty-six, had been knocked down as he walked home from a pub on the A6 outside Oadby. He was killed instantly. The car had not stopped and police were searching for the hit-and-run driver who they thought might have been over the drinking limit, since the incident happened not long after closing time. The late Frank Smith drank a beer or two in the pub in question on most evenings, although less frequently of late due to having been made redundant from his job at a printing works.

It wasn't a long cutting. Two or three inches. I didn't suppose he'd qualify for an obituary, so that was all the verbiage that the departure of the resentful Frank Smith would be likely to merit.

But why send it to me?

'No,' I said to Penny, in answer.

'No? You didn't know him?'

'No.'

Her eyes widened. With Penny I have a certain reputation. Penny always expects the worst.

'But,' she said, gesturing at the pieces of paper, 'then why – ?'

I smiled at her, even though I have to confess that my heart had tripped a beat or two; I don't like these coincidences. Nor could I understand why I had to be sent the cutting. The note would have been enough; I didn't need the evidence. It was as though Brooks was anxious to prove something: his truthfulness, perhaps.

'Nothing to worry about, Penny. Just an item for my scrapbook.'

Her brow furrowed. Her face froze. Penny hates to be kept out of things. Things, by Penny's definition, cover almost every conceivable aspect of the working and private life of everyone in the building. If I were to explain a single part of the circumstances in which I met Mr Frank Smith it would be round the building like a flash. The very fact of my meeting him would be counted as a contributory factor to his demise.

44

I said nothing more.

Penny drew herself up. Her brow furrowed even deeper.

'You're wanted,' she said. 'In fact, you're late. For the Art Fund meeting. Remember? They're waiting for you.'

6

'The most important thing,' Jeremy White said, from the other side of his shiny mahogany table, 'is not to panic.'

He did not look very confident as he said this, even though Jeremy, with his striking blond hair, his height and natural presence as a member of the White family, albeit a relatively young one – mid-forties is callow youth to the aged Whites – would, to the inexperienced outsider, have looked in full, positive command.

'Absolutely,' said Geoffrey Price, from my side of the shiny mahogany table.

We were not discussing the Art Fund. Not yet. It was the situation in general that was the preoccupation. You may not have noticed, but the mid-nineties has not been the most encouraging time for merchant banking, or investment banking, as the Americans call it. There has been the Barings business. Warburgs. Kleinwort Benson. Massive losses by some of the famous Americans like Salomon Brothers and Bankers Trust. Share price collapses like Merrill Lynch. Takeovers by massive high-street banks or foreigners. The atmosphere has been anything other than bland. White's Bank is not big and the wash from these events was causing it to bob about on the tumbled waters like a cork on the ebb tide. It is a relatively old bank, founded on the South American timber trade in times when things were less instant, less electronic. Jeremy has done great work in bringing it up to date, but the earthquake conditions of international finance are making life hazardous for the few surviving merchant banks in London. All the pundits forecast their demise or

46

their inevitable ingestion, in swift gulps, by large stock banks of varying nationalities.

Jeremy was looking at me expectantly. Some supportive reaction, like Geoffrey's, was clearly expected.

'God,' I said, 'as ever, is on the side of the big battalions.'

He scowled deeply. 'I hate it when you say things like that. These military analogies grate on my nerves.'

I ignored the frown but changed analogy. 'He is not always omnipotent. Small furry animals seem to survive whilst elephants trample the jungle and uproot the trees. If the said furries are fleet of foot and adaptable.'

'Very ecological.' His voice was not so much dry as arid. 'Very sage, I'm sure. We at White's Bank are not a species to live off the smashed particles left after the elephants have stripped the foliage. It would involve considerable diminution of our size.'

I nearly reminded him of the massive lay-offs that several investment banks had recently announced. Not hundreds of employees but thousands were being shed. Caution prevailed, however. This was not a time to upset Jeremy with such statistics; people in business, like people anywhere, can only absorb limited numbers of messages about reality. Reality is for zealots. There is also the distinct possibility that the said business people will take pot shots at the messengers.

'We're pretty lean as things are, Jeremy. If anyone can survive, we can.'

'Hear, hear,' said Geoffrey, not so much in approval of the situation but because, I recalled, he had recently been grumbling about what he had to cope with, considering the inadequate staff allocated to him.

There was a slight mollifying in Jeremy's expression. 'That may be so. But it will not help us if, in the mad scramble to get a decent share of a diminishing level of trading activity and investment funds, we lose out to these absolute maniacs from abroad, cutting margins and poaching as hard as they can.'

Now there spoke your traditional City man, despite Jeremy's maverick reputation. The old City man lived off very comfortable margins, margins which financed a leisurely pace and luxurious lifestyle. He regarded his patch – the entire financial establishment of London – the same way a landowner does his coverts or his rivers. Outside competition was considered no better than the tattered poacher with snare, net and fowling piece.

'Come, come, Jeremy,' I reproached him. 'The City is doing remarkably well against the competition. It's been a bit shaky of late but the overall performance is impressive. The expertise is first rate, the world knows that. Since the shake-ups we're as good as anyone anywhere.'

'You're right! You're absolutely right! Some of the foreigners are taking a frightful drubbing. We mustn't get into self-pity. It's harder to make a living but we can do it. It's just that one gets weary of living with constant pressure, constant sniping, to adapt your military expressions, from distant trenches. I know that out in the Far East they think of us as a lot of lazy, stuffy old has-beens, but by God I'd like to see them keep up with our pace for a few years. Knacker the lot of them, it would.'

'For sure.'

He was looking considerably brighter. Jeremy tends to move from ebullience to despair and back again with a volatility not associated with your average Anglo-Saxon banker. Not for him the gravid demeanour, the pinstriped, charcoal solicitude of the man behind the partners' desk. With Jeremy it is all dash and enthusiasm or it is disaster of a major order. He manages to get enormous excitement out of what many people would see as a pretty boring sequence of events. I'm not talking about the City wheeling-dealing of the TV programmes, the knife-edge, double-or-quits Nick Leeson-cum-Singapore activities of Barings hyperbole. Most of White's business has been comparatively cautious by the standards of such people, even though risk, sometimes pretty big risk at that, is the essence of merchant banking. At White's the directors like to know what's going on, who's dealing, and whether there are still fifty-two cards in the pack. Which is why, to many of the old gang, Jeremy started off as a figure of fear.

'In this country,' he now said portentously, warming to a

more positive mood, 'we have some of the finest talent in the world.'

'Indeed we have, Jeremy. Which prompts one to ask how it could come about that a flashy chancer like Piers Hargreaves got the job at Christerby's?'

For a moment I thought he might choke. A congested flush spread up his cheeks and his eyes popped white as they bulged at me.

'Tim! That is the most rampant red herring you've sprung for months!'

'Red herring? I thought we were freewheeling generally about the business before we got down to the Art Fund. I should have thought that Piers Hargreaves's appointment was of as much interest as any aspect of the business. Particularly since I have been so blatantly snubbed over the matter.'

Jeremy gaped at me in real disconcertment. Geoffrey Price stifled a grin, coughed and looked curiously in Jeremy's direction with a look that clearly wondered how our boss was going to field this one.

'My dear Tim! Snubbing does not come into it. Just because we – or rather the bank – is a shareholder in Christerby's, there is no reason for the Art Fund to be involved in such choices.'

'Not the Art Fund, I agree, no. But I am a non-executive director of Christerby's. No one asked my opinion.'

'Er, well, possibly not. Mainly because you are, after all, on the board to – to, er, represent the Art Fund interest in such matters.'

'Am I? There's no one else from White's on the Christerby board. Just me.'

'I am well aware of that.'

'So I do not represent the bank's interest? That's odd, because –'

'Tim, there is no need to be *pedantic* about such matters. You must be quite well aware that the bank can make its opinions, er, *known*, without necessarily firing away publicly at Christerby's board meetings.'

'Firing away? I have never, ever, *fired away*, as you put it, at any board meeting.'

49

'No, no, of course not. I'm not suggesting you have.'

'But I am merely an ornamental presence, then?'

He flushed. 'You're so *touchy* today. I would hardly describe your presence as *ornamental* in any circumstances. Quite the opposite, in fact.'

'Oh, how kind.'

My voice had gone very acid. Geoffrey was grinning broadly at this oblique reference to my broken nose.

'My dear Tim, your contribution has been invaluable. But in matters of this sort, as I'm damned sure your experience will confirm, there are other, er, other considerations and influences, as it were.'

'Which in this instance excluded me. What does Uncle Richard think about it all?'

As I may have explained, Jeremy's uncle, Sir Richard White, is an ex-chairman, having resigned following an intervention by Jeremy and me which was rather unpleasant at the time. Since then we have patched it up and although he has semi-retired down to the Dordogne, where he produces very passable wine and visits the battlefields of the Hundred Years War, he is still a strong influence on the main board. My recent foray to France to assist Maucourt Frères in an industrial assessment was at his behest. Things happened while I was away that were inexplicable; I couldn't see Richard approving of Piers Hargreaves.

Jeremy bridled at this introduction of a senior family member into the discussion. His life has been spent circumventing such *éminences grises*.

'Richard was not present when the decision was taken. He is, as you are well aware, almost completely retired, despite your continued and regrettable association. He could not be contacted at the required moment. He was probably at Crècy or Agincourt or somewhere, measuring arrow trajectories in relation to the speed of carthorses loaded with men in tinplate.'

'Ha!' I ignored the sarcasm. 'I thought so. I'm not surprised. He wouldn't approve. And anyone could have told you that Piers Hargreaves is a four-star, fur-lined, ocean-going disaster.'

'Tim! And then you wonder why you weren't consulted.'

'There isn't a company he's been in that hasn't shipwrecked in some way or another.'

'He specializes in difficult situations. The difficulties are not of his making.'

'If that's the case, what the hell is he doing at Christerby's?'

'You know very well what has happened to the art market in the last few years. Things may be on the mend but the rigging mustn't get slack. The ship's company needs to be spruced up. Put through its drill. Ballast must be shed.'

'That's already been done.'

'To some extent. To some extent. What is needed now is a firm hand at the helm. A captain who'll get things shipshape and Bristol fashion.'

Jeremy is a yachtsman. He can't help using these dismal marine images. But I'd got him on the defensive, I could tell that. There was a guilty look about him that betrayed hidden knowledge.

'At what cost?'

He bridled. 'Cost? Cost? What do you mean, cost?'

'Piers Hargreaves normally charges a fortune to bugger up good companies. What's the deal at Christerby's?'

'My dear Tim! I am not privy to his personal contract. But I've no doubt that full disclosure of directors' earnings will be made as a result of the normal, properly audited procedures.'

'Oh yeah?'

He flushed. 'What? What are you suggesting?'

'I'm just jealous. I wish I had Hargreaves's friends in high places, with their easy options in other firms. All I know is that a small investors' club I sometimes have to deal with automatically sells the shares of any firm to which Hargreaves is appointed a director.'

'Tim! Are you serious?'

'Perfectly. And I agree with them.'

'He did a marvellous job at Wappinger's.'

'Marvellous. Look at them now. Import everything from Hong Kong and Singapore, don't they?'

'Bergendale Press?'

'A shambles. Cut to the bone for a year to boost profits. Half

51

the workforce thrown out. The chief accountant committed suicide. Threw himself off the roof or something. They now need massive investment to avoid closure. He really does have the long term at heart, doesn't he?'

'Sarcasm ill suits you, Tim. It's perniciously negative.'

'All I want to know, and so certainly does Charles Massenaux, is how the hell he got this job and why? What's behind it?'

'Charles? You've been talking to Charles?' A look of suspicion as deep as Sue's had come to his face. 'Why? What for?'

'Jeremy, Charles is an old friend of mine. It is quite normal for him to express his concern to me. Naturally he thinks, he *thinks*, that because of my position I was involved in some way in this appointment. He expected me to have some explanation. My position is very embarrassing.'

'Ah. Well. Yes. Perhaps. But Charles must know that this sort of, of very senior appointment involves far more than, than –'

'Meets the eye?'

'Tim! That is enough! Quite enough! We have wasted much time already. I am sure Piers will soon make the benefit of his experience plainly evident. He is very experienced and the choice was not made lightly. This discussion is now ultra vires. We must stick to the matter in hand.' He turned towards my companion, making it clear that the Hargreaves file was now firmly closed. 'Geoffrey; have you the agenda for this Art Fund meeting?'

'No,' said Geoffrey, bless him, without expression.

'No? No? Why not?'

'Because this is an informal review meeting.' Geoffrey is one of your calm, cool accountants who plays Sunday cricket with a legendary straight bat. It takes a lot to shake Geoffrey. 'We only have an agenda at official trustees' meetings.' He smiled a winning smile. 'If you remember, you said we must cut down on paperwork.'

'Oh. Did I? Well, I suppose we must listen to Tim's verbal report, then. At least, if not a report, an update. Tim?'

'We have bought nothing since our last review meeting,'

I said. 'As we agreed, we thought it best to keep our powder dry until the market looked more positive. It is possibly a good time to consider an acquisition, if a really good opportunity arises, since we have some cash and there may be some paintings in our category well worth buying. However, there hasn't been anything really exciting for a while. Sellers are holding back until things improve. It's all still a question of confidence.'

'I see.' Jeremy sounded quite disappointed. 'So you weren't talking to Charles about anything specific?'

'No, Jeremy. Just an update. The main topic was Hargreaves.'

He pursed his lips. 'We can't remain inactive for ever. There must be some opportunities about. I've been much too busy with other matters to look round myself.'

'All of us have been busy, Jeremy. Art has had to lie at anchor, awaiting a fair wind. It's been a case of all hands to the pumps just now.' I smiled ingratiatingly. 'If you'll forgive the boating analogies.'

'You are a snide bastard, do you know that?'

'If you say so, Jeremy.'

'This is all camouflage. Smoke screens. I suppose you're about to go off and buy something really choice, aren't you?'

'I never make major decisions without consulting the trustees, Jeremy.'

'You'd better not.'

'When have I ever?'

'You're on to something. I can tell. You've got that beady, shifty, smug look about you.'

I grinned at him. 'I can't think what makes you think that, Jeremy.'

'A sense of horrible, impending doom. What is it?'

'Jeremy, I have seen no work of fine art that I can recommend to the trustees as a desirable purchase.'

'Ha! A typically evasive answer. Come on: cough it up. Who are you thinking of?'

For a moment I hesitated. I'm usually very open with Jeremy. But he hates Cubism, Abstraction and Modernism. Picasso is a dirty word to Jeremy. What is more, the other members of the main board, a bunch of sheep, are always asking why we don't buy the Impressionists. That, coupled with Jeremy's love of pretty pictures with blue skies, green fields and accurate feminine figures, is always a problem.

'Tim?'

Clearly, he wasn't going to give up. Resignedly, I kept my voice even, matter-of-fact. 'I am considering Wyndham Lewis.'

I might just as well have stepped on his toe. He let out a strangled yelp then goggled at me. 'What? Vorticism? Can you be serious?'

'We have an Art Fund which specializes in the best works by modern British artists, from approximately the mid-nineteenth to the mid-twentieth century. Lewis is a key twentieth-century figure. In 1914, Pound, Joyce, Eliot and Lewis were said to be the key men of culture. Despite the recent return to favour of the peripheral Bloomsburies, he cannot be ignored. Now would be a good time to buy.'

'He was a filthy fellow. Wrote absolute tripe. Fascist. Misogynist. Lecher. Cubist. Diseased with the clap.'

'Sounds like the makings of a top-rate painter,' Geoffrey said, with a sly grin. 'Move over, Van Gogh and Toulouse-Lautrec.'

'Geoffrey! *Et tu, Brute*?'

'Those are some of the common misconceptions and some of the facts,' I said. 'It remains, however, that his painting work is exceptional.'

'I regret to say I am aware of his standing amongst certain art historians. Do you have a work in view?'

'Er, no,' I lied. 'Not yet. I am merely considering a concept.'

'If I know anything, that means that the police will need to get out reinforcements.'

'Jeremy, I find it distressing that you, and Charles, and Sue, should take up this attitude.'

'There you are! You have been discussing it already! You dissembler! You mole! I knew it.'

'Only in concept.'

'Oh dear.' He affected a weary sigh. 'Geoffrey, we must prepare for the worst. There will be no stopping him, though,

54

despite any advice we may offer. Advice to Tim is water off a duck's back. I suggest we need refreshment. Come on; if there's nothing else to report – as though this were not enough – let's all go and have lunch.'

Geoffrey nodded enthusiastically. If there's one thing that binds we City men together, it's the thought of a good lunch.

'Good idea,' he said.

'Excellent. And over the table we can grill Tim on just how costly and potentially criminal this latest fad might be.'

'That,' I said, 'is quite unnecessary. It is not a fad. And I have acquired by far the major part of the Art Fund's assets without the slightest hint of trouble of any kind.'

I nearly added that I had no doubt that the quest for a Wyndham Lewis would prove as uneventful as the other, major part of the acquisitions, even if one person had been strangely struck down already. But that would have been much too rash. The gods hear remarks like that, so I kept it to myself.

Although, by definition, gods can read minds, too.

7

The board room at Christerby's is half-panelled in brown mahogany, above which cream walls sport forbidding portraits of past directors, their features composed into the pained, undertakers' expressions suited to the making of money by the disposal of other people's goods. I strolled in with ten minutes to spare before a board meeting and found myself, unexpectedly disconcerted, facing two very different men.

'Ah, Simpson.'

The chairman, Sir Hamish Lang, is a crusty old trout who has always regarded me as too young, too poorly connected and too irreverent to be taken seriously as a board member. His approach to my presence varies between superior condescension and downright disapproval. The latter is preferable. To him, I am an unnecessary imposition by White's Bank, whose Art Fund he regards with the unconcealed distrust of one whose family provided him with suitable works of art long ago and who can't imagine anyone investing in paintings and such in an abstract sense rather than buying a Raeburn or a Peploe of their own.

Sir Hamish, as you might gather, is a Scot of originally West Highland family origin, but you wouldn't guess it if you met him without prior knowledge. Like so many Scots brought up with almost both feet in England – educated at Winchester and Trinity – he looks, sounds and acts like a classic English gentleman who has inexplicably acquired a palate for porridge and kippered whisky. I say almost both feet because, in addition to his flat in town and a Berkshire mansion, he has a property up in Scotland somewhere, doubtless turreted in granite and surrounded by inhospitable moorlands noted for their wet peat, wet heather, wet bracken and wet, but moving, wildlife targets. In appearance the small, white-haired Sir Hamish has looked like a pretty fit hundred-year-old ever since I've known him, and will almost certainly still look the same twenty years on. He is thin, spotlessly clean, aquiline, acquisitive, sharp as a razor and tailored to a standard I'll never live to afford.

'Simpson,' he croaked unenthusiastically, looking me up and down doubtfully and crooking a bony hand in my direction, 'I'd like you to meet our new managing director, Piers Hargreaves.'

I moved obediently towards the pair in front of me, not quite tugging the forelock but contriving, I hoped, to produce an expression that combined a friendly, open countenance with keen anticipation at the pleasure and honour about to be bestowed.

'Piers – this is Simpson. Er, Tim Simpson. Of White's, you know. One of Jeremy's men. He is, of course, a non-executive member. Simpson, I thought you should meet Piers Hargreaves, who we have been fortunate to persuade to join us.'

'So I gather, Sir Hamish.'

I just managed to keep the irony out of my voice as I shook hands with the new supremo himself. To my surprise, he had toned down his normal Flash Alf appearance by wearing a pinstripe that wasn't in broad chalk lines like a bookie's and a soft silk tie patterned quietly against a striped shirt with a white collar. He might have been a successful estate agent rather than the stage impresario he normally emulated. As I anticipated, he was large, taller than me in a commanding fashion and fair – almost blond but not as blond as Jeremy – with a broad brow, long pointed nose, keen eyes and a humorous, cruel mouth. His frame was heavy under carefully styled coverage, so that the impression of power and influence was marked.

Leverage, I thought, this man can exert leverage, like that bastard in *The Great Gatsby*.

'My goodness,' he said, shaking hands firmly with me. 'I've been looking forward to this.'

'Oh?'

'Tim Simpson. *The* Tim Simpson. I've admired your and Jeremy's Art Fund collection for a long time.'

'Really?'

'You bet.' He'd abandoned the hectoring bray I associated with him and spoke quite normally, in a deep but pleasant voice. 'To have got that lot together in so short a time is a real achievement, quite apart from the investment aspect. You've caused a lot of envy in some quiet exalted museum and gallery circles, you know.'

'Oh? No, I – I didn't know that.'

'Come, come, you're too modest. White's Art Fund is regarded with real admiration by some very important people.'

Sir Hamish was looking at him incredulously.

'You're familiar with the content of Jeremy White's Fund? His investment affair? I didn't know that.'

There was an affirmative nod. 'Indeed I am. Intimately. Ever since I was a trustee at the Sherringham I have envied the range, the brilliant representation of modern British art it encompasses.' His expression became didactic. 'Any fool with money can go to auction and buy routine paintings of the Modern British school. The trick is to acquire the right works at the right price. The exploits of this young man are quite legendary.'

Sir Hamish Lang's lower jaw dropped open. He gave me a disbelieving stare, which I almost reciprocated. I was beginning to feel more than distinctly uneasy. There was something terribly wrong about all this. I had formed a quite definite view of Hargreaves as a pompous menace, yet here he was, doing his best to be as pleasant and as flattering as possible. Not only that, his whole manner and appearance were in sharp contrast to his behaviour every time I'd seen him on TV. It is true that the so-called celebrities or public figures seen on the idiot's lantern are far more human in the flesh, but I was really surprised –

A thought occurred to me.

58

'Well, that's very kind of you, er – '

'Piers, please. Tim. Piers.' He grinned to show shiny teeth. 'We're fellow directors now.'

'Piers. I'm sure I don't deserve it. And it's not as though your own exploits have gone, um, unnoticed. Welcome to Bond Street. I was talking to Charles the other day – he's not here yet – and he was telling me about your plans to, um, raise the profile of Christerby's by using TV – '

'Ha! He's told you about it, has he? The Medallion programme? Excellent! I know he seemed a bit diffident but I think he'll be great at it, don't you? I'm afraid I wouldn't take no for an answer. I believe he's exactly the right man. What do you think?'

I looked Hargreaves in the eye. I had to incline upwards slightly to do it and I'm not short. 'As a matter of fact,' I said, truthfully, 'Charles will be brilliant, once he's got the hang of things.'

Another dazzling if somewhat wolfish smile lit up his face, causing further unease to our chairman's expression. 'Oh, marvellous, Tim. I'm so glad you agree with me. I took one look at him talking to a prospective client who'd brought in a minor Cezanne and I thought: that's my man. He was superb. Not too abstruse but technically perfect and absolutely comprehensible. The client handed the thing over like a lamb. Charles will be first rate. We'll have to watch that he doesn't do an Arthur Negus on us or something, I can tell you.'

I grinned at this. The idea of Charles as a modern Arthur Negus, ruminating amiably over a Hepplewhite chair or a Staffordshire dog, was too great an imaginative leap to take. Charles is a smooth cove, not a screen folk figure.

'I don't think Charles is cast in quite that mould,' I said.

'No, I don't either. In fact, he's better for today's television. The amateur has yielded to the professional, not that Negus wasn't professional, but he was too homely for today's environment. I'm sure Charles'll cope with TV far better than I can. I hate the medium. Makes me horribly nervous.' His vulpine smile broadened. 'Always find myself banging on

59

about things I never intended. Opinionated, too. Nerves, I suppose. What about you?'

'Can't say I've ever had the pleasure.'

'Really? I'm surprised. I should have thought you could do a marvellous programme on the Art Fund.'

I gave him a slightly alarmed stare. The last thing I wanted was to appear on Medallion TV at the behest of one of Piers Hargreaves's chums or as a result of a sly suggestion to Jeremy, who would probably wax enthusiastic about the idea whilst remaining firmly off screen himself. I put the thought away quickly; my real concern right then was the contrast between the Hargreaves I'd seen on TV or read about in the papers and the man I was talking to now.

'I don't think that's my forte,' I responded feebly, wondering how I'd deal with the threat if it strengthened.

Fortunately a rather nettled Sir Hamish was keen to intrude.

'Very interesting, very interesting, but we mustn't ramble on,' he pronounced, already adapting to a chairmanly mode. Clearly, he wasn't enjoying the concord in front of him. 'Work to do, all of us. Meeting's due to start. Glad you've met, anyway. Excuse us, won't you, Simpson? Must get on; others are arriving – here they are. Got the agenda, Frank?'

This last was to Christerby's company secretary, spreading papers on the table. He nodded patiently and winked in my direction. The room was filling with other directors. Hargreaves smiled at me and moved off with his chairman to the ruling end of things while I wandered downwards to my post below the salt. I found Charles Massenaux at my elbow.

'I see you've met the great man,' he murmured as we seated ourselves. 'Our Leader's quite the sober dresser today, ain't he?'

'Positively funereal,' I murmured back, 'compared with what I've seen before. Pleasant, too. I can't think what's gone wrong.'

'New wife.'

'Eh?'

'New wife, dear boy. Brand new, only one week out of

the box. Country girl, not an ex-actress like the previous two. No more dramatics; it's all horses now. Dun coats and green wellies. Dropped the Jag for a Range Rover Discovery. Understatement's the order of the day. Pity really, because she's rather a sweet thing. Wasted on him.'

'Good heavens! I wondered what on earth had changed.'

'Country air. Place up in Northamptonshire with trees and landscape.'

'She's had quite an effect.'

'Watch it, Tim; he's at his most dangerous when being pleasant.'

'Well, you never know what a nice girl might do for him, Charles.'

'It'll not last.'

'Charles, Charles. We must hope for them both.'

'Not a chance. Theatricals are his natural métier. Blondes with bosoms, preferably bare. Dramatics. Declamations. Our Leader. Bottoms up; frilly knickers. Not a beams-and-four-poster man at all. Centrally heated apartment's more his mark. He'll not like groping under the freezing bedclothes to get a grip on her – '

'Charles! *Please.* The chairman is glaring at us.'

This was true. Our whispers were holding back Sir Hamish from starting his preliminaries. He was making an ostentatious display of waiting for silence, with an arctic stare in our direction.

Charles subsided, but for a few moments I got the giggles. His fantasized, irreverent reference to actresses and knickers had reminded me that, according to a theatrical ex-wife's expensive Sunday-paper revelations, Hargreaves had required her to wear just one such frilly undergarment and nothing else whilst engaged in dramatic frolics of domestic felicity. It set me off. I got out a clean handkerchief whilst Sir Hamish introduced the new managing director and pretended to blow my nose whilst still repressing mirth. It's not often humour intrudes at one of Sir Hamish's meetings and I determined to make the most of it while the vapours lasted.

They evaporated fairly quickly.

Our chairman wound his tedious way through the previous minutes, points arising, that sort of thing, with several pedantic references back to the secretary. Hargreaves sat confidently awaiting his moment. There wasn't anything for me – mere voting fodder today – to contribute. In a swing of mood, I started to feel bolshie and resentful about both Sir Hamish's attitude to me, and Jeremy's, their lack of concern and the way Jeremy didn't disagree when I said my presence must be just ornamental. The non-executive fee was paid straight to the bank, not to me. I hadn't got very much of an ethical responsibility. There was no margin in listening too hard.

They hadn't even bothered to have the courtesy of asking me my opinion about Hargreaves, even if they intended to ignore it. It was grossly rude; the matter still rankled.

Bugger them, then.

Charles's recollection of Hargreaves's whimsical sexual stimulations got me thinking of a story of Wyndham Lewis, • rogering his landlady's daughter in the hallway when the post was delivered through the letter slot and envelopes fell on his bare buttocks. My mind wandered divertingly on this theme – you never know where your correspondence may end up – until I shook my head, blew my nose again, and tried to blot out the disturbing images.

'Piers has some very interesting ideas on spreading our wings from the pure auctioneering role,' I heard Sir Hamish say.

Hargreaves leant forward, his appearance bringing to mind the profile of Sir Osbert Sitwell so brilliantly derided in Lewis's novel *The Apes of God*. There the luckless aesthete appears as Lord Osmund Finnian Shaw, a man the colour of pale coral with flaxen hair, malignly called a pencilled pap, rising straight back from a sloping forehead. Lord Osmund's nose could not, in Lewis-language, simply flare; it had galb-like wings and made his profile goatish, as befitted a man dedicated to wine, womanry and free-verse-cum-soda water.

But there was no free verse or soda water about Piers Hargreaves. Womanry, that was another matter. There you might say he followed the goatish description pretty well, which was more than dear Osbert ever did; in that allusion, Lewis must have had his tongue in his cheek.

Wyndham Lewis; he was bound to fill my reveries. The drawing of Iris Barry was now safely at home for Sue to see on her return. Four days had gone by. I still couldn't fit those four men together. Well, there were only three of them, now. Nor could I work out, if they were setting me up for a scam of some sort, how they were planning to do it. So if not, what had I got to lose?

The mind quickly rationalizes things. I decided they'd come to me because it was obvious. In Britain, White's Art Fund would be the place to go if you were determined to avoid public auction. It was a question of contacts, too; people like George Welling wouldn't know where to start with the Mellon or one of those North American galleries.

Although Brooks might.

Piers Hargreaves started to talk, mellifluously and calmly in his deep, new, unhectoring voice. The influence of a good woman is inestimable. I thought of Sue, back home tomorrow. She'd like the drawing of Iris Barry. Maybe there wasn't a painting, large or important. If there was, we would have it authenticated before any money changed hands. I'd got nothing to lose. Art acquisitions have been made in much more bizarre circumstances. Mr Brooks and his companions might be ill-matched but they weren't exactly bohemian. Mundane, commercial, working sorts of men.

There was something not right about it all, though. Something odd. I tried to work out what it was, but the nub eluded me. The men just didn't seem to fit together, somehow. Yet what possible purpose could they have?

Piers Hargreaves started to talk about communications. Charles gave me a nudge. This was his slot, or his proposed slot. Hargreaves actually mentioned him and the forthcoming Medallion programmes. The other board members turned to look at Charles, who blushed a comely pink. There were murmurs of congratulation. Someone said something about a new rival to the *Antiques Road Show*.

Charles smiled in wintry disbelief.

After he went blind in 1951, Wyndham Lewis did quite a

bit of broadcast work for the BBC. It was radio stuff, adaptations, working with a man called Bridson. For someone in Lewis's condition it was a life-saver, but his wife tried to commit suicide that year. The irony is that when he was young, in 1914, he said that when you hear that a famous man is dying, penniless and diseased, you accept that part of life's arrangement is that the few best of us become these cheap scarecrows. For him the prediction came all too true.

My mood was turning sombre. The disturbing images were no longer sexual ones.

– 'just a broad indication of strategic thinking at this stage' –

Piers Hargreaves was still banging on about communications and had thrown education into the pot as well. His voice was starting to boom in the way I'd heard on TV. I found myself frowning. The worst thing an auctioneer can do is to lose sight of his role as scavenger and marketplace for the transfer of wealth, property and resources. The PR men like to play the educational card and there's quite a lot to do, if you fancy it, in publications and videos, that sort of thing, but it's pretty ancillary. Mind you, the BBC have become a ferocious publishing concern, using their visual advantages to the maximum they are allowed. But they aren't auctioneers.

They did need some competition, though. Maybe Hargreaves was right.

My mind was wandering.

– 'more detailed and concrete proposals to the board fairly soon' –

When could the painting have been done? Wyndham Lewis's art output slowed down soon after the First World War. He was disoriented and disillusioned. He got flu and double pneumonia. He'd done more than his bit at Passchendaele and then as a war artist for the Canadian scheme, while others like the Bloomsburies stayed at home, claiming to be pacifists and massaging their contacts. His career had stalled. His mother died. His father's inheritance was taken from him. No wonder he felt persecuted. In 1923 he took to writing rather than painting and didn't go back to art for quite a few years.

– 'highly confidential at the moment, of course' –

Piers Hargreaves was now adopting an intimate, man-of-the-world tone, presumably to make we followers feel part of a process over which we had no control –

It's interesting how often, once the excitement fades, people take to writing. Dick Francis. Margaret Thatcher. Plenty of them. They rarely do it while the hunt is on, but Lewis, novelist, philosopher, critic, always a painter, could waste magical language on his tinpot targets.

If the painting was pre-1919 it'd be terrific. If it was from the 1919 'Guns' exhibition it'd be terrific, too. It might be from one of the 'Tyro' exhibitions. Even if it was one of the later ones it'd be great. Big and important –

I realized I'd just missed something more Hargreaves was saying about a broad strategy for future investments and integration. I should have been listening. If I'd been listening properly I'd have got the coded messages which, when my mind was normally clear and sharp, I'd have decoded quickly and jumped to verify. My oar would have gone in immediately.

But I was thinking of Wyndham Lewis, and Notting Hill, and was sulking about Christerby's, so I didn't. I let it slip by.

Hargreaves stopped talking and the meeting ended. I said cheerio to Charles, wished him luck with the filming and left without analysing what had just been said or making the necessary connections.

Which was both stupid and neglectful of me.

8

I'd promised Sue I wouldn't go to the Tate or the Imperial War Museum and I didn't. There wasn't any need to. Those Cubist pieces at the Tate wouldn't tell me anything I didn't know already and the gallery's famous lampoon-portrait of Edith Sitwell, turbaned, gawky and morose, with coloured tubular squares in place of hands, must surely be imprinted on every art lover's brain. She actually told friends that she ceased to sit because Lewis made a pass at her; about as incredible a story as anyone could invent.

In the same way, the huge canvas of *A Battery Shelled*, with its odd jagged smoke and the bulbous background flash of the eponymous explosion was familiar to me already. It's a staggering painting when seen in the flesh, odd and bemusing and advanced in a way that might irritate if it didn't call to a deeper sense within the viewer. The three casual figures to the left, the fellow artist Wadsworth among them, the injured stick-figure of a man being carried off, the almost incidental, almost distant howitzer itself, the spaces; it takes some looking at, that painting. Nowadays Paul Nash is held to be the king of the First World War painters because he's so easy to understand, so emotionally horrifying. People tend to move away from Lewis's difficult version of things. That's always the problem with Lewis; nothing about him was ever easy. He was unforgettable in conversation when he wasn't brooding in silence; I would love to have met him, just once.

I suppose my character and background stem from the kind of man Wyndham Lewis most affected to despise. When I am not being pugnacious or truculent or am off on my own joyful little excursions I try to be good-humoured, democratic, liberal, unintellectual, sporting, mildly iconoclastic, usually irreverent. Some of these are the anti-vital-Oxbridge attributes of what Wyndham Lewis described as a feminine and exhausted culture, representing the dregs of Anglo-Saxon civilization. There is nothing softer on earth, he said in his novel *Tarr* in 1918, than an average specimen of the Cambridge set: 'a cross between a Quaker, a Pederast and a Chelsea Artist, its flabby portion being a mixture of the lees of liberalism, the poor froth blown off the decadent nineties, the wardrobe leavings of a vulgar bohemianism with its headquarters in Chelsea.'

It's strange how we've managed to survive at all.

To Lewis, the English national characteristic of good humour was anathema; he said that it helps to project a comforting mediocrity which avoids individualism and blurs the inequalities of nature, providing the illusion by which the English disguise the cruelty, indifference and ruthlessness of real life. The isolated, malign laughter of Lewis, whose belief in the need for a tiny minority of geniuses to rule the great lumpen mass of conformist humanity led him to admire Hitler for a while, had nothing in common with our good humour, despite the testimony of men like Julian Symons – a most un-Lewis, semitic figure, with his deft, intelligent conversation, Marxist-anarchist perspectives, humanism and lettered, intellectual tolerance – that Lewis, in person, was charming and brilliant company, even if Lewis, in print, was a savage.

He was also a rotten judge of character. Worse, his brilliance led him to fight with all the wrong people. When he was old he said that if he had known what damage Roger Fry could do to him he would never have denounced Fry in public over the Omega Workshops affair, even though he, Lewis, was in the right. The greedy, self-promoting Fry and his friends kept Lewis out of everything, every single bit of patronage, public or private, that they could, ever after.

Being the sort of Englishman I am, it would be easy for me to put Lewis's problems all down to the influence of the European Continent. Dictators are what the Continent produces; along with many others in the twenties and thirties, Lewis liked intellectual brilliance and power, the idea of men above the herd, of dictatorships.

We don't.

The Saxon is not like us Normans.
His manners are not so polite.
But he never means anything serious till he talks about justice and right . . .

A spell in Madrid with Spencer Gore, then on to Paris, Hamburg, Munich, Holland and Brittany, studying Bergson but approving much more of Nietzsche doesn't make for an offshore islander. The weak and the strong, the sick and the healthy, art versus Connolly's pram in the hall; those were the opposites with which Lewis treated over and over again. Six crucial years on the Continent implanted the authoritarian, hard-edged attitudes so instinctively avoided by an amiable fudge-country, all watercolours and cultural caution until it is roused.

Until it is roused.

When he stands like an ox in the furrow with his sullen set eyes on your own,
And grumbles 'This ain't fair dealing', my son, leave the Saxon alone . . .

For some reason this line of thinking, as I taxied my way back to the bank after my resentful session at Christerby's, had me thinking of Piers Hargreaves. Behind that amiable approach there had to be some sort of purpose, some reason for him to be so friendly. Men on the make like Hargreaves are naturally cold and calculating; if I was to become a pawn in some Hargreaves game I should become alert, but to what? I clearly didn't figure in any calculations of Sir Hamish Lang's; Jeremy was playing his cards close to his chest; I'd been away in France when something or other involving Hargreaves went on which must have involved the bank. I had an uneasy feeling; Sue would be back that evening, which was nice, but I had an uneasy feeling. Hargreaves's record, so far, was one involving change, usually unpleasant change. Charles's warning rang in my ears –

He's at his most dangerous when he's being pleasant . . .
Well, maybe, Charles, maybe; here was one Cambridge man whose culture was neither feminine nor exhausted.

As Sue would surely confirm.

9

It is extraordinary how interruptions occur first thing these days. The early morning isn't sacrosanct any more. There was a time when a man accosted at breakfast could be expected to lash out at any approaching intruder and such behaviour would be understood, even perhaps approved of.

It isn't like that now.

There is something about the finishing of breakfast that brings out my philosophical side. As I sit at the table by the long window overlooking Onslow Gardens, contemplating my tea while Sue sips her coffee or reads the paper, knowing that I am preoccupied and therefore silent, I often find that my mind wanders in consequent but tangential directions to the project in hand, like an explorer who sees the heights he will have to scale distantly in front of him but is concerned, or maybe diverted as he moves along the foothills, by a novel theory of escalation that has just occurred to him.

So it was the morning after Sue's return. She said she'd had an interesting visit to Glasgow; the curators had all rabbited on about their favourite problems and subjects and the social side was good, but she seemed vaguely discontented. Sue is normally a very straight, efficient sort of curator, holding down a coveted, responsible and interesting position at an early age. We have been happily settled and married for long enough to anticipate each other pretty well. If I have introduced phases of danger and fear, we have overcome them together on more than one occasion. She has had to teach me to think about her before plunging too far beyond my depth, but she's never held it against me. From time to time I have to keep her in the dark during the early stages of my art pursuits, but I would never exclude her entirely. It's just a question of timing. I had a feeling, however, that she was now going through a reassessment phase. So far so good, her mind was thinking, but where do we go from here? A woman would say that it was an intuitive feeling; I just caught the odd look from time to time. The sort of look that disturbs a man, takes his mind off the novel theories of escalation and undermines the icy resolve that men like Wyndham Lewis can use to eliminate anything that they see as an enemy of promise or a diversion from artistic or intellectual exercise.

The weak, the pram in the hall: I took a careful look at Sue as she put down the paper and turned her querying eyes upon me.

'What?' she demanded.

'Wyndham Lewis believed,' I answered over my teacup, 'at the time he wrote *Tarr*, that women should be relegated if art were to be served properly. Sex was something the intellectual should go slumming for, not raise to any level of his own. Woman, therefore, was a lower form of life unless of male characteristics.'

'Charming. The family was pretty low stuff too, I seem to remember, by the same logic?'

'Absolutely. All that woman is intended for, according to him.'

'Is that how he justified chucking away his five illegitimate children?'

'Good question.'

'Not exactly a model for modern man, was he, Tim? But I think you forget that his wife always said what wonderful company he was.'

'Wives are so forgiving.'

'Tell me about it.'

'I will, I will. But when or where have you been reading about Wyndham Lewis's wife?'

'Froanna? My dear husband, you are always so maddeningly condescending. I was fascinated by Wyndham Lewis when you were still chasing a ball about a muddy rugger field.'

71

'My apologies. Abject ones. Put that down to male arrogance. What conclusion did you come to?'

'On Lewis? Oh, that he was undoubtedly a self-destructive genius. I'm not very *au fait* with his writings but on his painting I have no doubts. He was way ahead of anyone here. Our first abstract painter, one who never got stuck in a rut. One who has philosopher-intellectuals still arguing over his published work in droves. I'm very pleased that you've decided to buy him for the Fund, despite the inherent violence, the clash of his vision.' Her expression became sly. 'I feel that your artistic development shows signs of encouraging progress at last. I take it that although your reading is clearly well under way, you still haven't got a painting in view?'

The question was put in a sharper tone of voice and I was conscious of a more intense scrutiny as I ignored the schoolmistressy judgement on my backward artistic condition. On the other hand, my mind, still working in philosophical mode, was still taking in the concept that if my wife accepted the conclusions of genius arrived at by Lewis, to what destination did that lead a marriage?

'Er, no. I'm still following one or two leads where a painting is concerned.' I moved a nonchalant hand towards my teacup. 'But I have acquired a drawing.'

'A drawing?' The reaction was as sharp as I'd hoped.

'Yes. Of Iris Barry. Possibly a study for *Praxitella*. Would you like to see it? I hid it in the bureau last night.'

Her jaw dropped. 'Tim! You mean you bought a Wyndham Lewis drawing, brought it here, and didn't show it to me when I got back from Glasgow?'

'Er, no. I didn't.'

'Why on earth not?'

I didn't answer. She stared at me for a long moment and then slowly a slightly disapproving but mischievous smile moved her lips just a fraction. Her voice became inquisitorial.

'Let me guess: you hid it from me because you had other, less intellectual priorities in prospect. Didn't you? You thought that if you showed it to me I would be diverted into speculations about what you're up to that might postpone the undoubtedly unintellectual, lower-plane activities you intended and which, as things worked out, you were able to practise. Am I right? Look me in the face when you answer.'

'How devastatingly well you know me, Sue.'

'You're disgraceful. There is nothing worse than low cunning of that sort.'

'Wasn't such bad thinking, though, was it?'

Her mouth compressed briefly. 'No, as a matter of fact, it wasn't. I'd never have – I'd have been – I wouldn't – oh dear, how well you know me, too.'

'The result wasn't so terrible, was it?'

'Don't fish for self-satisfaction. I hate seeing you look smug.'

'I am not looking smug.'

'You will if given half a chance. Let me see the drawing.'

I got up, took the drawing out of the bureau and put it in front of her. The sharp penetration of Lewis's view of Iris Barry sprang at us from the paper. Sue turned her head one way then another before nodding approvingly.

'I'd love to own this. So often drawings are much better than a finished painting. Where did you get it?'

I had prepared an answer to that. 'From a Midlands auctioneer. Or rather ex-auctioneer who's an agent now.'

This was technically true. With some economy of information, however, I felt it unnecessary to mention that one of his collaborators had almost immediately been squashed by a motorist near Oadby, Leicester, at pub closing time.

Sue nodded again without further query at the apparently unremarkable source. 'When do you want to come and see the paintings at the Tate? There's only one on view now: *Workshop*, in Gallery fourteen. The others were taken down yesterday for a new exhibition.'

'There's no hurry. I –'

The telephone interrupted me. With a shrug at Sue's querying expression as to who it might be, and a feeling of irritation, I went across to the bureau and answered.

Jeremy's penetrating tones pierced my ear. 'Tim?'

'Jeremy?' A frisson of nervous anticipation went through me. Unless there was a disaster, Jeremy used never to

73

phone me before I left for the office. I had not allowed for the unpleasant early-morning trend I've mentioned. His voice boomed at me in a way I felt might be influenced by our new eminence at Christerby's.

'Tim, the most remarkable thing. I've just been chatting to Piers.'

'Hargreaves?'

The boom turned testy. 'I don't know another Piers.'

'Sorry.'

'It seems that he's a most avid Wyndham Lewis fan. Extraordinary, isn't it?'

'*What*? Jeremy, have you been discussing the Fund with him?'

'For heaven's sake, Tim, don't be so *parochial*! Piers is part of the scene now! Naturally we have much in common. There's a lot of *synergy* to be developed between us and Christerby's which it seems to us both we've been missing out on.'

'Thanks very much.'

'Oh, stop it! He spoke of you in the most flattering terms. We went on to talk about the Fund's acquisitions as a matter of course.'

'Oh, my God.'

'What on earth is the matter? For heaven's sake, Tim, I'm trying to *help*. You and Geoffrey are getting to be terribly *blinkered*. Piers has asked us all to a party at his flat tonight and he'd love it if you and Sue can come and see his Wyndham Lewis drawings. He's been a fan for years. He could be a mine of information. I've phoned you now so that you can catch Sue before you leave. Can she come?'

I clamped a hand over the receiver.

'Sue?'

'What is it?'

'Party? Piers Hargreaves. Tonight? To look at his Wyndham Lewis drawings?'

'How super.'

I took the hand off resignedly. 'Very well, Jeremy. Sue says OK.'

'Excellent! Tell her well done. Thank heavens one can rely

on someone. And try to be enthusiastic, will you? There could be splendid contacts, you know.'

'Yes, Jeremy.'

'See you at the bank later.'

'Yes, Jeremy. And Jeremy?'

'What?'

'I'm pleased to hear that you've come round to Wyndham Lewis after all. Especially in view of our new, um, colleague's enthusiasm.'

There was a moment's seething silence. Then he said: 'You are an absolute bastard, do you know that?'

'If you say so, Jeremy.'

I put the phone down. The last thing I wanted was a dominant Piers Hargreaves stamping his big feet all over my territory. At the back of my mind I suspected there were all sorts of things, City things, going on that no one wanted to tell me about, which would affect my life in some unpleasant way or another. I wished, now, that I'd paid more attention at the board meeting.

Too late.

Sue got up and came across to straighten my tie, getting her face close to mine. 'You look dreadfully glum. What's it all about?'

'I wish I knew. But Hargreaves is up to something and Jeremy's in it with him.'

She smiled wickedly. 'I've read a lot about Piers Hargreaves. It'll be interesting to meet him. What do you think his fascination is? For all those wives and others?'

'Money.'

'Tim! I do believe you're jealous. Just because he's so obviously a rampant, chauvinist male. There are always takers for one of those.'

'He's a shit. I don't know why he's cultivating me – or maybe us – but he's still a shit. With money.'

A look came into her eye. 'Wealthy shits are so often very attractive,' she murmured. 'And a challenge, of course.'

'In that case I'd better start –'

'No. Not you, softy. You'll never make a successful shit.'

'How kind. Naturally, I respect your judgement. I have to

go. I'll come back here before the party, so we can go together. OK?'

'OK. Where are you off to?'

'First the bank. Then I'm going to a dress rehearsal.'

'Theatricals? A dress rehearsal? For what?'

'For a TV programme. Into which, reluctant, but certain, I think a new star is about to be drawn.'

10

An ominous telephone call came through not long after I arrived at the bank that morning. My secretary Penny is a county girl of respectably limited career ambitions but an abundant social life, which she pursues enthusiastically, provided the young gentlemen wishing to escort her have suitably elevated educational and family qualifications or are rich. For this reason, her attitude to my callers is perhaps more critical than other secretaries of my experience. Penny is a severe filter; she does not like ominous telephone calls.

She phoned through to ask me if I would speak to a 'Mr Brooks' who would not state his business – 'He wouldn't say who he's from,' as she put it, rather tartly – and was silently disapproving when I said that I would, without explanation.

A male voice, somewhat lowered and furtive, came on to the line in an overconfidential tone I wouldn't have associated with the sharp-eyed little man of the studio in Notting Hill.

'Mr Simpson.' It was a statement, not a question.

'Mr Brooks.' I tried to keep my heart from quickening; what news of the Wyndham Lewis painting would he impart?

'I trust you are well.'

'Yes, thank you. You?'

'*Pas trop mal*, as they say across the Channel. I cannot complain. The funeral, the very sad funeral, of Frank Smith took place yesterday.'

'I was very sorry to get your note, Mr Brooks. Have they found the hit-and-run driver?'

His voice hoarsened a little. 'Alas, no. I fear he – or she – has so far escaped identification.'

'Oh dear. I'm sorry to hear that.'

'The police are continuing with their enquiries.'

'I'm sure.'

I tried not to sound curious, though I was. Someone knocked down and killed the miserable old codger. Why? Was it really an accident? There was no suitable motivation connected with me that I could discern so far, but I wasn't convinced this was pure coincidence, not going on past form. What possible role could Frank Smith have been expected to play? Why was it necessary to eliminate that role?

'Frank's was not a happy life. He had many trials to bear. In a way, though it may sound unfeeling, a quick end can be a mercy, Mr Simpson.'

'Er, yes, I, um, suppose so.'

I said this as I wondered whether, if asked, the late Frank Smith would agree.

'We must carry on though, as Frank would have wished. I thank you for the very prompt delivery of the cheque. A receipt is in the post to you. Now, some matters concerning our recent, interesting exchange have come up on which I would like to elaborate. But this medium is uncongenial for the purpose. I prefer to talk to you in person. Is that possible? Today?'

I hesitated, finding the natural question that sprang to my lips a bit difficult to suppress. Brooks, however, as he had in the studio, anticipated my thoughts.

'I am sure you are anxious for news, but the matter is a little delicate. There have been some developments but one cannot be too careful on the phone. This is a local call, so it is not likely to be logged by the authorities at Cheltenham in the way they do international ones, but one never knows. Eavesdropping has reached epidemic proportions everywhere. Does your organization normally record all incoming calls?'

'Good heavens, no.'

'Good.' He sounded not so much relieved as approving. As though we had passed some sort of test. 'Many companies

78

nowadays are prone to such intrusions. Surveillance, in our modern society, is out of hand. Experts have perfected the electronic ear and long-term recording equipment to an extent of which the general public has no conception.'

'Oh?'

'Yes. Especially where financial organizations are concerned.'

'I – I see.' Once again, I didn't, and the subject was so removed from what I wanted to talk about that I had to clench a fist round a thick pen so as to relieve my tension.

'Does your secretary have a line to us now?'

'No, she doesn't.' I heard my voice shortening. 'My secretary never listens in to my conversations.'

I wished I could be certain of that as I said it; with Penny, one could never be one hundred per cent sure.

'Excellent. Forgive me for asking. I hope I do not offend. It is what I would expect of you, though, Mr Simpson. In your situation, with your investments, a policy of absolute confidentiality must be essential.'

'It is.' The sooner we dropped this extraordinary subject, the better. 'Would you like me to come to Notting Hill to meet you? To your studio? Is that what you'd like?'

'No, no.' His reaction was quick. 'That will not be necessary. Thank you, but I do not need to drag you so far.'

'I have to go to Bond Street shortly. It's not so much further on for me.'

He did not comment on this information; his reply was smooth, as though ignoring it or perhaps even expecting it. 'May I suggest the Cleveland Arms in Paddington? Chilworth Street; it crosses Westbourne Terrace. At lunch time? Rather suitable, given the circumstances. We can, I think, meet there confidentially. Unless you object? Is it likely that there will be colleagues, or business acquaintances utilizing the place, who might recognize you?'

'No. At least, it is highly unlikely. But –'

'Good. The Cleveland Arms, then. Chilworth Street. At, say, quarter to one?'

'OK. If you wish. Is there –?'

But he had rung off already, leaving me to the sound of

my voice and the tension of my nervous suspense, alone in my office in the bank, in Gracechurch Street, in the City of London.

11

For the dress rehearsal they had fixed up a space at the back of the basement of the auction rooms, with fairly minimal floodlighting and a backdrop of muffled furniture. This was an episode they planned to do before they went on the road to various centres where Charles was to pontificate in local galleries and provincial rooms of the Christerby's network. The idea, as I understood it, was to look sometimes at permanent collections and sometimes at goods brought into local auctions, or on sale at local markets, with the basilisk eye of a Bond Street man whilst listening to his Delphic pronouncements. It could not help but be a very personal affair, in which success or failure would depend almost entirely on the presenter.

To record these tableaux there were surprisingly few camera crew and hangers-on – I supposed that any company associated with Hargreaves would have its staff cut to the bone – and nothing like the amount of cabling and paraphernalia I visualize when people talk of filming. No one paid the slightest attention to me as I picked my approach to the back of the group.

I had deliberately avoided the start of events because I thought that my arrival might make Charles nervous, so found that he was finishing off a rather worthy description of a small, Pre-Raphaelite painting of a wan lady in blue by a chap called Smetham, who I remembered was a faithful follower of Rossetti and eventually went right off his rocker, which was par for the course if you were a faithful follower of Rossetti. Charles was talking competently but, whether from nerves or whether from residual and resentful resistance to the whole idea, he wasn't the Charles I knew he could be when confronted by an article to spark him off. Stimulation was lacking.

As I slipped in quietly at the back of the group watching intently, he finished his little dissertation with an apposite quip and the chap directing events stepped forward to approve. I got a surprise; it was Mike Watson. I recognized him at once; when I was up at college he was a great Footlights man and we'd known each other tolerably well. This certainly couldn't be the 'poof of a producer' Charles had mentioned with such venom; in my day, Mike was a dedicated ladies' man.

'That's good, Charles,' he called out. 'You're starting to get the hang of it splendidly. Could we now try the walnut chest there, to establish a balance from a painting to something a bit more three-dimensional?'

Charles nodded cautiously and turned to a rather badly proportioned eighteenth-century walnut chest of drawers parked nearby. The cameras swung obediently and there was a certain amount of hoo-ha whilst the sound equipment was checked, then Charles put a hand on top of the chest and began his spiel.

'Here,' he said, in a clear, reliable voice, bending tolerantly over the veneered surface but still without real spark – Charles is not much of a furniture man and I made a note to warn him or Mike Watson about that once they'd got their focus or whatever they were fixing – 'we have a typical eighteenth-century walnut chest of drawers with a quarter-veneered top, which is repeated on the surface of this brushing slide' – he tugged at the tiny brass pulls under the top moulding to extend the slide towards the cameras – 'which was used, so it is said –'

'Stop! Hold it!' Mike Watson's voice cut him off in an order responding to a cameraman holding a piece of video equipment of complex shape, who was signalling something frantic. 'Awfully sorry, Charles, but we've got a slight snag here. Won't take a moment; have a breather, would you?'

Charles nodded and stepped back a pace or so. I nipped

around the bods scattered between us and was alongside him in a twinkling.

'Tim! What on earth are you doing here?'

'Just popped round to wish you luck.' I stuck my lips close to his ear and lowered my voice so no one would hear. 'I liked the bit about the Smetham, but didn't he go barking mad?'

'Er, yes, he did.'

'Local colour, Charles. Personal touches. You should use them; they love that sort of thing. But I say, watch it with this horrendous chest, won't you?'

His eyes whitened wide. 'Why? What's up?'

'It's a modified press. East Anglian. Look at it. The proportion's all wrong. Someone's reveneered the top after removing the upper structural press part – you know, the screw tackle and frame – then they've inserted a slide because the top'd be too deep if you left it as it was. It's the standard trade treatment for converting those chests into saleable walnut, you know that. The brushing slide is much too high at that level. On a genuine brushing-slide chest it's much lower; how else would you use it to brush your clothes on?'

'Jesus.' He stared at the top of the chest and the extended slide before us. 'You're absolutely right. I've been so preoccupied with the bloody cameras and the thought of this wretched programme I didn't look closely. It's a real dog, isn't it?'

'A howler. The quarter-veneered slide repeating the top must be wrong, too. At least, it's the first ever if it's right.'

He tamped down his sleek black hair with his characteristic nervous gesture. 'My God. I nearly made a real fool of myself. Thanks, Tim.'

'My pleasure. I'd take it easy on furniture if I were you; it's not really your thing, is it? I see you've got Mike Watson running the programme, by the way. I knew him at college. Good bloke. I don't think he's a – oh, hello, Mike.'

'Tim!' The director had come over to see who was chatting up his possible star. 'Tim Simpson! What a surprise. My God, what are you doing here? How nice to see you.'

We shook hands animatedly.

83

'Just popped in to wish Charles would break a leg.' I grinned at him. 'We're long-term friends and colleagues, Charles and I.'

'Good heavens. You old devil.' He looked me up and down. 'Haven't seen you for ages. You're looking well, considering. Married now, I hear.'

'Oh yes. You?'

'Five years. Two children. Absolute terrors. Boy and girl. Any little Simpsons?'

'Er, no. Not for the moment.'

'Well, well, well. Still under starter's orders, eh?'

'I was just telling Charles he's in good hands with you.'

'How kind. Look, I'm afraid we're holding things up a bit. Sorry to have to cut it short, but we have to work to a tight budget. Can we catch up with the gossip over a pint sometime?'

'Delighted. I'll get out of the way.'

'Thanks, Tim.' This was from Charles, who was manoeuvred back to the chest as I slipped behind the watching crew. There was a signal from Mike Watson, the lights altered somehow, the sound man moved forward, then –

'Here,' Charles said yet again, leaning confidentially to the camera this time, 'we have a typical eighteenth-century walnut chest of drawers with a quarter-veneered top, which is repeated on the surface of this brushing slide' – he did his slide-opening bit – 'which was used, so it is said, to brush clothes on.' He smiled significantly, crinkling his eyes at the corners and closing one lid just a little more than the other. 'How very odd, then, that the level of this slide should be so high. And how odd that its veneer should be exactly the same as the top. Extraordinary. I have never seen such a thing before.' His gaze to the camera became more confidential; his face was slightly flushed and excited. 'It is these little signs that started the alarm bells ringing in the mind. In antiques, so often all is not always what it seems to be; there are certain things to look out for, pitfalls to avoid. This is especially true of what are known as "trade improvements" intended to enhance value and no part of the original piece. Here we have a typical example.'

84

Across from the cameraman, I saw Mike Watson put finger and thumb together, remaining three fingers cocked upwards, in a sign of joy. Charles moved slightly backwards, then came round to gesture at the front of the chest.

'The press chests of East Anglia – '

He was good. I have to say that he was good. Whether the slight shock of my intervention had stimulated him, or the challenge of the duffed-up chest, or more likely the combination of the two, I'll never know. But he was off; definitely, enthusiastically away and going, his voice different, his manner alert, his attitude responsive. It ain't what you say that counts, it's the way that you say it. Charles has always had a streak of the thespian in him; here at last was his chance. He took that chest verbally to pieces in a display that was first class.

At the end of his peroration half the crew broke out into spontaneous applause. Mike Watson jumped forward with congratulations. Charles smiled modestly and tamped down his hair as a girl poked a dab of powder on a cheek. He beamed at her cheerfully. Mike Watson went back to the Smetham and brought it into the floodlights. I saw Charles point at it and start to talk animatedly. Watson grinned and started nodding.

I slipped back upstairs and out into the bustling light of a busy Bond Street in order to grab a taxi.

Charles was well and truly launched on his new career which, as if in retribution for my smug but well-meant assistance in helping it along its way, was to have an impact as telling on me as poetry and films had on the characters sending me those messages.

12

Whenever I turn out of Paddington station on to the wider
end of Praed Street, I am tempted to divert my way into the
narrow, eastward canyon of low commercial activity which
crouches under St Mary's Hospital to reach Mr Goodston's
bookshop, where many a biographical tome and art-related
memoir stands dustily shelved, awaiting my arrival. This
time, however, my attention to Charles Massenaux had left
me only just on schedule for the Cleveland Arms, so I managed to be strong and turned the other way, up Craven Road.
Apart from Mr Goodston, from whom I have obtained much
of my library, there is normally no reason for me to be in
that strange region of boarding house and seedy hotel, that
shifty hinterland north of the Bayswater Road beloved of
Wyndham Lewis. Not that he would recognize much of it
now; it is being subjected to creamily painted stucco restor-
ation in sporadic, scaffolded outbursts, like white-chocolate
icing spread over patches of flaking, eczemaed architecture.

Today I had good reason to be there, reason that made my
step smarter, my movements taut.

Once over Westbourne Terrace, with its marching bow
windows to watch the streaming traffic, and into Chilworth
Street, you perceive the ranked facades of Cleveland Square,
almost as tight and classical as the upper Faubourg St Honoré.
Here the once individual front doors of what were originally
meant as houses seem to have been hermetically sealed into
a solid phalanx, the better to shelter the secretive flats into
which the mass has been divided. What goes on behind those
dead-windowed, moulded lineaments cannot be discerned;
in daytime, no inner life stirs their solemn exterior.

The Cleveland Arms in Chilworth Street is an unstuccoed relict of dark London stock brick, its frontage a glazed high bay on either side of which open, angled doors beckoned. I strolled in cautiously to find a bare-boarded grey floor, sparsely spotted with high stools at raised, small, uncomfortable pub tables. Down the left-hand side of the room, in front of brown half-panelling, were conventional rectangular wooden tables, each equipped with menus and four single wheelback Windsors of recent vintage. A row of flags hung above them: I counted two Union Jacks, the Stars and Stripes, two Irish tricolours, a Welsh flag, two European Unions, but no Scots. A TV video thrummed loud disco music and a well-dressed young West Indian was playing at a pin-table machine. At the bar, three workmen in paint-spattered overalls sat communing over pints, presumably between bouts of cream-surface camouflage outside.

There was no feeling of comfort or cosiness of any kind; I was in the shell of an old London pub with a dark lincrusta ceiling, its guts ripped out, its back room fitted with an American pool table, its walls, where not black-boarded with messages in coloured chalks about all-day breakfasts or beers from Germany and Mexico, decorated with spoof-sepia photos of Cockney barrow boys and whelk vendors from some long-historic other-life, gravid under a rotating brass punkah-propeller made in Taiwan to chill the draught from the open doors. As a symbol of modern London – but no, I mustn't start that.

I bought a pint of John Smith's bitter – my grandfather was a Yorkshireman – and strolled over to one of the side tables where there was a fair view of the length of the bar. Anyone coming in through the doors would certainly be visible to me as they entered or, at least, I'd see them within a pace or two of entry. My punctuality might well have been a reflection of my anxiety; Mr Brooks's clandestine manner had simply stoked the pent anticipation I was bottling in over the prospect of an exciting acquisition for the Fund. I took a cautious sip of the bitter and tried to sit back, looking casual; my feelings were anything but.

The bar was not full; at one end two suited men were

unenthusiastically ordering hot food from a barmaid who was either Australian or some form of Cockney variant; from my distance the twang was hard to identify properly because the disco video from the small screen boxed on high had moved to a scene of oscillating black girls for whom the volume automatically jumped up a notch. There was no sign of Mr Brooks anywhere.

One of the paint-spattered workmen gave me a quick appraising glance, one that said you don't belong here at this time of day, mate, this place has been stripped so that your sort can pack in and yah-yah whilst standing over spritzer-stimulated office girls after work, all of you jammed together and shrieking with watered wine. I picked up my straight glass and looked back at him steadily but without aggression; he went back to his conversation.

Quarter of an hour went by. I hadn't told anyone about this visit, either. Something about Notting Hill was causing me to be even more reticent than usual.

Thinking over Mr Brooks's furtive manner that morning reminded me of a TV programme I'd seen about the logging of international phone calls; had he been watching, too? Why the worry? What paranoia pursued him down the electronic wavelengths? Or was he just, for the sake of atmosphere, imitating Wyndham Lewis's persecution mania, the one that made him sit in cafés with his back to the wall and tell people there was someone at a nearby table listening to everything he said? That kind of aberration lent credence to the rumour of mental decay caused by syphilis.

Another quarter of an hour went by. Still no sign of Brooks.

A lady called Lynette Roberts wrote a poem, sometime during the fifties, about the woman who infected Lewis, though who she was and why that should have stuck in my mind, heaven alone knew –

Another quarter of an hour went by. My glass was empty. I was still alone.

More ruminations; more minutes ticked by. Lewis lived right across the street from this pub for a while; there is a story of sending out for a bucket of beer for Roy Campbell, poet and friend, on one of his visits. Was that why Mr Brooks had chosen it? I looked at my watch for the umpteenth time. Past two; much too late for him to be coming. Something was wrong; something was very wrong. Prickles began to needle their way down my back; my stiff knee, legacy of a collapsed scrum at Twickenham, starting to throb the warning it always throbs when a sense of danger comes upon me.

The delay might be something perfectly explicable; a traffic jam, a relative taken ill, a business crisis.

Chance would be a fine thing.

That's the trouble with acquisitions for the Art Fund; they have the ability to bring up images of the worst, the very worst, that can happen. You start to believe things like Mr Brooks dead, murdered, stopped from meeting me because of some terrible revelation, or the greed of a partner or associate. It's the first possibility that comes to mind. I concentrated for a moment on that ill-assorted quartet: Brooks as neat as a rat, Welling rather fat and useless, Macdonald silent, a hard, fit, sardonic sort of man, Smith rheumy, defeated, lost – no, not lost: dead.

One dead, how many to go? I still hadn't dared to tell anyone else about Smith; I could imagine what they'd say. Was Brooks to be next? I couldn't phone him; I didn't have a number. For whatever reason, his first contact with me had been to ask if I'd come to Notting Hill.

I could remember the conversation on my office phone that day exactly; Penny was taking a day off and the operator put Brooks straight through.

'Mr Simpson?' The unknown voice I heard then was precise, educated. 'You don't know me, but I am calling you regarding your Art Fund. A possible acquisition I think might very well interest you.'

'Oh yes?'

And then he'd talked of a Wyndham Lewis painting. It was a most opportune moment to catch me. As though he'd timed it to the day. Something lying dormant, some residue of the Nevinson affair, embers still warm, were kindled. Images flashed across my mind. Why hadn't I got round to Wyndham Lewis before? For the major Slade painters, the collection was complete in many ways: Brown and Tonks themselves, the Johns, McEvoy, Orpen, the Spencers, Nevinson, Carline, many others. Why had I so neglected Lewis? The call was a reproach.

He gave the Notting Hill studio flat address, agreed the meeting time and rang off before I could get a phone number from him. In retrospect, it was odd, even risky; how could I have advised him if I had to cancel? How did he know I was certain to come?

Where the hell was he? Had something terrible happened to him?

It was no good staying rooted to the spot.

I got up, left a note at the bar to say that I was headed for the garden studio in Notting Hill in case Brooks arrived, went outside and hailed a taxi. I sat stiff as a poker on the back seat as it rattled round the back of Paddington, cutting through on a parallel to Westbourne Grove, then across Pembridge Villas. We got to the back of Notting Hill much faster than I'd hoped. In no time at all I had paid off the taxi and was striding down the lane between the terrace-ends, with their sealed map-cracks like rivers, to reach the garden –

The card had gone.

It hit me just as I was about to ring the bell by the door in the yellow-black wall. The card neatly printed with No 42B, Garden Studio, with its arrow, had gone from its place on the wall. Opposite, the wrinkled card for 40A, basement flat, was still there, like a tart's invitation to join in subterranean sordidity.

I rang the bell, staring back up the lane to make sure I wasn't mistaken. No one passed by in the street beyond. I might have been in a voided village. The card had gone.

There was no answer. I rang again. Over the top of the gate I could see the pergola with its vine and ivy forming the leafy tunnel to the hidden studio. Beyond that rose the roof, with its skylights set in the slates.

Still no answer. I rang again.

At last, a car went past along the heavily parked road at the opening to the lane. It was reassuring. Life was still going on, normality existed. My sense of loss, the anxious desolation that was mounting, abated a little. Brooks must have been detained somewhere, was out on business that had delayed him, would contact me, all apologies, when I got back to the bank. I decided to leave him a card; there was a letter slot in the gate for mail –

'Hello.'

The voice was female, oldish, with a definite Cockney twang to it this time. Bewildered, I looked round.

'Up here, dear.' The voice rose in pitch.

I looked up at the bulk of the house to which the studio was attached and saw a grey-haired, portly woman in a pink overall coat leaning out of a first-floor sash window.

'Hello?'

'They've gone, dear.' The voice was matter-of-fact, not unsympathetic.

'Gone? Who? I'm looking for Mr Brooks.'

'They only took it for the week, dear. It was the studio you wanted, was it?'

'Yes, but –'

'Just the week. I don't know the name, but I understood they only took it for the week. I do for the flats here, you see. Clean up and that.'

'I – I don't understand. You mean this studio is let by the week?'

'Well, for longer, dear, if they can. But it's quite expensive so they don't get long lets much.'

'So Mr Brooks was only here for the week? I came here about a week ago.'

'That's it, then, isn't it? He's gone now. I did the place over yesterday. They left it very neat and tidy, I must say.'

'But –'

'What, dear?'

'Nothing.' I felt like a fool, deflated, idiotic. 'Thanks.'

'That's all right. Haven't you got a forwarding address?'

'No.' A thought struck me. 'Who does the lets? Who handles them?'

'The agents, dear. By the tube station at Notting Hill Gate.' She named a well-known firm. 'You'd have to ask them.'

'I see. OK. Thanks very much.'

'You're welcome, dear.'

The sash closed. I went back down the lane and into the road, mind seething as I strode rapidly towards Notting Hill Gate. What the hell were they playing at? Surely the whole thing hadn't been set up just to sell me the drawing of Iris Barry? That was ridiculous; it made no sense at all.

I bought the Iris Barry cheap. I haven't admitted that yet, have I? But I did; I'd have paid more. Wyndham Lewis drawings, depending on the subject, go for anything between two and eight thousand, even at auction, and Iris Barry is a good subject for a gallery or a Lewis fan. All that sycophancy of Welling's was a load of moonshine. I'd been sold the thing cheap for a reason. Something was definitely wrong.

At the estate agent's office I drew a helpful woman who looked as though there wasn't much business going on. She remembered Mr Brooks well but gave me an anxious look when I said I wanted to get a forwarding address.

'I'm not sure we're meant to give away details of the clients,' she said. 'And I don't think, from what I remember, that our reference would be much help to you anyway.'

'Oh? Why not?'

'He paid cash in advance. Nice man, I remember. We've not had that many takers for the studio recently so we were rather glad to get just a week's rental. Normally it's by the month. We took a deposit cheque in case of damages but he collected that back a day or so ago. You've not missed him by very much.'

'But didn't he give you any address at all? Surely you have to have that?'

'Yes, of course. But' – she looked into the brown manila file on her desk – 'he said he was in London for a brief period only. So it was a sort of forwarding address. Like a poste restante. With full payment in advance it wasn't so important. He filled in the form for me himself.'

'A forwarding address? What sort of forwarding address?'

She looked at me apologetically. 'I don't see there's any harm in giving it to you. Hardly very revealing; it's the Pall Mall Depository.'

'The what?'

Her eyes widened at me. 'The Pall Mall Depository? Care of the Pall Mall Deposit Company? That's what's written here. In Pall Mall. Actually – I have to admit – I can't say I really know of it. Why – what's the matter?'

I set my startled face back to normal. 'Nothing. Nothing at all.'

I didn't tell her that the Pall Mall Depository doesn't exist. Not any more. If an estate agent doesn't know that, or can't be bothered to check it, why should I let on? I didn't tell her, either, that it was once one of Wyndham Lewis's most famous secluded addresses, a fugitive facade designed for disappearance. I moved to leave as decorously and as quickly as I could. There was no point in explanations. Nothing useful would come from the estate agent's file. Mr Brooks, quite clearly, not only had a sense of humour; he was as secretive as Wyndham Lewis himself.

And as absent.

13

Piers Hargreaves's 'modest London place', as I had heard him call it, was a flat in St John's Wood, on the northern edge of Regent's Park, in a modern block almost overlooking the zoo. The interior was modern too, and might have given an impression of expensive lightness and space if it hadn't been full of well-dressed people, all talking animatedly. There was a high level of noise and a distinct shortage of elbow room.

'My God,' Sue said, as we entered, 'the place is packed.'

'Home life with the Hargreaveses,' I murmured. 'Jeremy reckons he entertains most nights.'

A white-coated waiter offered us a tray of drinks. Sue took champagne, I took a red wine. We hesitated for a moment, but Hargreaves was an assiduous host, I'll say that for him; he was before us – resplendent in navy pinstripe, fresh white shirt and scarlet tie – within seconds.

'Tim! Welcome, welcome. So glad you could come. And this must be the celebrated Sue. So delighted to meet you, Sue.' He leant over her with an appraising, admiring stare. 'When I was at the Sherringham, the Tate crowd were full of your praises.'

Sue managed to simper very slightly. 'I'm sure that's not true.'

'Absolutely! I can assure you.'

He grinned at us both wolfishly. The Tate is so like the Civil Service in organization and attitude that I couldn't imagine any such personal praises being sung, but under its thick pink skin Hargreaves's expression betrayed no sign of dishonesty. Whether flattery was a normal part of his

94

weaponry I didn't know, but in both our cases he was using it lavishly.

'The Sherringham? It's a marvellous collection, but they seem to be having a tough time of it just now,' Sue responded, perhaps mischievously.

His expression changed rapidly to one of anxious concern. 'I know. I know. I'm really very worried. One hoped, when one left, that things were back on an even keel and that expansion could be managed without this overheating and loss of revenue. But we live in difficult times for art establishments, don't we?' He leant closer to her in a more confidential manner. 'Have you seen this evening's papers? About what the Lottery's giving its money to now?'

'I –'

There was no time to respond properly to this propinquity and rapid change of subject because a rather pretty woman, considerably younger than Hargreaves and simply dressed, had come up to stand beside him. He moved back, looking slightly disconcerted.

'I don't think you've met my wife, Eleanor, have you? Ellie, darling, this is Sue and Tim Simpson, of whom I'm sure I've told you great things.'

The girl was dark and tall, about Sue's height, and the two of them shook hands with responsive smiles at each other. I shook hands too, and was also smiled at the same way.

'I'm going to show them the Wyndham Lewises, dear. Could you hold the fort for a few minutes while we go into the bedroom?' He grinned wryly. 'I did see that it was respectable in there earlier on. I'm looking forward to both their opinions; Sue is a curator at the Tate and Tim runs White's Art Fund.'

'In that case,' his new wife said firmly, 'I'm coming with you.'

He raised his eyebrows tolerantly. 'Very well, dear, but we mustn't leave our guests for long.' He grinned meaningfully. 'They'll think we're doing a foursome or something.'

His wife frowned fleetingly at this lamentable lapse of taste, but only shook her head slightly in reproach, as though such a thing was so far from possibility that its suggestion was

95

beyond the absurd. Sue had no expression at all; her eyes looked briefly into mine without a flicker. We nudged our way through the chatter, with Hargreaves having to stop frequently to exchange banter or salutations, and eventually reached a short passage which led away from the living room and on to three or four doors which presumably were bedrooms and bathrooms; evidently the kitchen was on the opposite side of the flat.

Hargreaves threw open a door to reveal an airy bedroom with a king-sized double bed in it, otherwise conventionally furnished, with many built-in cupboards or wardrobes. A few clothes were thrown on the bed, but the general impression was tidy. On the spacious walls there were quite a few prints, drawings and watercolours. He stopped to our left and gestured grandly at a line-drawing portrait head of a woman, a sudden strange glitter coming to his eye.

'There she is.' His lips quirked in a small, cruel smile, and his voice became recitative, like a master calling a roll. 'Myra Viveash. Lucy Tantamount. Margot Metroland. Iris Storm. Ophelia Dawson. Mrs Charlemagne Cox. Baby Bucktrout. Or Brigit, from one of George Moore's books I've forgotten the title of; some say he was her natural father.'

There was a pause as we stared at the portrait.

'It was *Ulick and Soracha*,' Sue said, calmly, into the silence.

'Good heavens.' Hargreaves stared at her, startled. 'That's absolutely right.'

'Drawn by Casimir Lypiatt,' Sue said. 'From *Antic Hay*?'

'That's absolutely spot-on too.'

The drawing had the unmistakable lines of a sharp Wyndham Lewis portrait. I stared at it in wonder, absorbing Hargreaves's extraordinary memory for all the literary characters inspired by the woman depicted in front of us. Michael Arlen, Aldous Huxley, Evelyn Waugh, Richard Aldington, George Moore, Wyndham Lewis himself; not a bad line-up of authors for a woman to claim to have inspired, even if not necessarily with approval. Nancy Cunard didn't sleep with all of them as well as her procession of non-literary lovers, if lovers is the correct term for an additional succession of quick couplers, just Arlen, Huxley – who, she said, was pretty lousy: 'like being crawled over by slugs' – Aldington, Lewis – 'magnificently brutal' – and another writer, Louis Aragon. Lewis chased her to Venice, after which they had a row; up till then, the only drawing I'd seen of her by Lewis – a cloche-hat flapper sort of image – had St Mark's campanile in the background. It was some time afterwards that a jealous Huxley put Lewis into *Antic Hay* as the failed artist Casimir Lypiatt, whose machine-like forms spray across his canvases with diagonal, demonic energy. It was a strange revenge for their rivalry over Nancy Cunard because even the fictional Lypiatt remains faithful to his art and Lewis was certain of his own significance but perhaps he didn't mind; he was always lampooning real-life characters in his own fiction and to have appeared in Huxley as well as novels by Osbert and Edith Sitwell, D. H. Lawrence, James Joyce and Lawrence Durrell must inure a man to literary cartoons.

Hargreaves was still peering at Nancy Cunard. 'Extraordinary woman. She certainly got around. Had a black lover, too. Very advanced for her day.' Hargreaves didn't actually lick his lips while speaking and staring at the portrait, but visually the impression conveyed was disturbingly similar; a moistening of the mouth was so apparent that he almost seemed to slaver over the cold, inked lines. His speech filled with saliva. There was a moment of silence as we all looked at this interpretation of the celebrated socialite before he shifted himself a foot to the right, breaking his concentration with a shuffling movement.

'And who's this, do you think?' Rather excitedly, he indicated another portrait head, almost alongside the angular Cunard, as though seeing it for the first time. In reality it must have been a daily sight. He fixed us with a stare that came first to me, then rested on Sue. 'A little test for you both. See how *au fait* you are with Lewis's ladies. I bought it without attribution, just as a signed Wyndham Lewis sketch, but I think I've a pretty good idea who it is.'

The glitter was once again evident as he switched back to me then returned to Sue. I saw another drawing of a long-nosed female face, no Cubist edges this time, rather softer in rendition: heavy-lidded eyes, wide mouth, an enigmatic,

97

almost Slavic look. Sue moved closer to both Hargreaves and the drawing, smiled faintly and looked at me queryingly, eyebrows raised.

'Ladies first,' I said gallantly.

'You know who it is?'

'I think so.'

'Clues?'

'A muse for another artist. Around 1906 or 1907, I think?'

'That's a bit broad. Nothing more specific?'

'Very artistic, but actually a secretary at the *Illustrated London News* for about fifty years?'

Sue nodded approvingly. 'Clever Tim. Yes, I think it's Alick Schepeler. Almost certainly. Augustus John painted and drew her prodigiously until she went off to Cumberland on a sketching tour. Wyndham Lewis's turn came round about 1915.'

'Bravo! Bravo both.' Hargreaves grinned broadly, transforming the strange glittery look briefly before letting it return again. 'I'm glad you agree with me. I'm sure it's Alick Schepeler. German father, Irish mother. Born in Russia. Youth in Poland.' His voice thickened and he set himself slightly astraddle, legs apart, to face the drawing head-on. 'As empty-headed and pliant a beauty as any artist could ever want for a model. Silent and obliging. The Janie Morris of her day. John was infatuated with her. Yeats too, I believe.' He peered more closely at the face, as though seeking to obtain something hidden from it. 'There's plenty of Augustus John versions of her; I'm afraid I lost one – another drawing – in my last divorce settlement. Maddening; it was done entirely to hurt; she didn't really care for it.'

His wife's face twitched darkly at these unhappy references, but I was engaged by a different thought his attitude and demeanour were suggesting. Did Hargreaves base his artistic purchases on a liking for scandalous background and relationships or for the article itself? There was an almost blatant voyeurism about the way he looked at the drawings, a stance, a set to his body, which was entirely physical. At first I didn't want to accept what it was. Now I knew what it reminded me of: the cocking of a dog's ears as it is excited by amorous intentions. For a moment he seemed lost to us, breathing a little heavily through the nose, watched by the sultry but impassive, almost lapidary face preserved in front of him, as though hoping it would animate itself in some tantalizing or stimulating way. I've always had an overdeveloped love of the biographically esoteric in art and can sympathize with any fellow fan, but this sight of Hargreaves had nothing to do with biography; it was somehow unhealthy and embarrassing, as though here, in his matrimonial bedroom, he was revealing hidden obsessions which were too personal, too deviant to be entrusted to casual visitors.

He was also very close to Sue. By some imperceptible, gradualist movement, he had closed the gap between them and the tension, the set of his posture as he looked from one drawing to another then back to her, was transmitting a body language of which I was suddenly, unpleasantly conscious. Hackles started to prickle gently down my spine.

'She had extraordinarily fine eyes,' Hargreaves said to Sue. As he said it, leaning closer, he put his hand in the middle of her back in a familiar, shepherding gesture.

'I think,' Ellie Hargreaves said, in a clear, unemotional voice, 'if you don't mind, Tim and Sue, you must excuse us. Please stay and look as long as you like.' She raised her voice just a fraction. 'We should get back to our guests, Piers.'

He almost started, his head flicking up and round to look at her. The hand moved away sharply. 'Of course. Of course.' The tension was broken. 'My congratulations to you both.' He stood back a little and looked at Sue in a more normal, easy manner. 'Especially you, Sue. You really do know your Modern British, I must say. You make a formidable pair.' He smiled at me as he said this, as though the inspection of the drawings had been nothing but a perfectly pleasant, normal interlude at a conventional cocktail party. 'And you can see that I heartily approve of your decision to buy a Wyndham Lewis for the Fund, Tim. I'm a dedicated fan. I'd love to have the chance of seeing the one you consider before you make your decision. Will you be involved, Sue?'

She shook her head quickly. 'No. I'm not part of the Fund.'

'But a major influence, I'm sure?'

99

The tone was once again flattering. I spoke almost sharply as I said, 'Of course, I always consult Sue. Without her, none of the really important acquisitions would have been made.'

'Very wise. It is a remarkable collection. You're a lucky man, Tim. I really don't want to intrude, and I promise I won't do it again, but Lewis is a passion of mine; please may I come for the ride this time?'

I must have frowned. 'Come for the ride?'

'Yes. It's your trip, your outing, but I'd simply love to come along. Whenever you get wind of a Lewis, I mean. Knowing you, it will be soon. Please?'

His manner was practically beseeching. Completely out of place for such a big, powerful man. I was badly disconcerted. Jeremy has always allowed me such latitude in the actual discovery of pieces, whether from mundane auctions or in more exotic circumstances that, apart from Sue, it has never occurred to me to take someone else along. Normally, explaining the presence of an outsider is awkward unless they are a specialist, like Charles, and their involvement tends to be well after the discovery, at the point of authentication.

That lunch time's events didn't help, either. There was no way I was going to describe my visit to the Cleveland Arms to anyone, let alone the discoveries at the garden studio in Notting Hill. Coming so soon after Smith's death, the void at the centre of my vortex was entirely my affair.

'Well –'

'I promise to behave.' He grinned boyishly. 'I know it's your show. But just this once? Please?'

My hesitation, in front of his wife and Sue, was looking churlish. I was conscious of looking inept. I was also much more conscious that this man was now very important to my work and position in some hierarchical sense not yet explained to me, and that despite my feelings about his just-past stance towards Sue, it was not the time for me to act naturally.

'Of course,' I said, with a smile. 'I've never been asked before, so I hope you'll forgive my surprise. But when I get a positive sighting, I'm sure you would be welcome to join me.'

'Oh thanks! That's great!' His face shone. 'Gosh, I'm glad I agreed to join Christerby's. It's going to be great fun. Sorry, Ellie is getting agitated about our guests; please do excuse us; we must continue our fascinating conversation later.'

He took his wife's arm and she smiled once, quickly, as they left us, leaving the passage door open. I found that Sue was looking at me with a long, assessing stare, eyebrows slightly raised, as we stood alone together in the abandoned, luxurious bedroom. The two portrait drawings hung impassively, but I found it hard to keep my eyes off them as I only half-returned Sue's stare.

'What?'

'Come on, Tim. I can read you like a book. Say it.'

'I don't need to if you already know, do I? But I will. That was very weird, wasn't it? Definitely odd. Or was it just me?'

'Go on.'

'These' – I gestured at the two drawings – 'got him going, didn't they? Turned him on in a distinctly marked manner? And you – I didn't miss that – he found you interesting, all right. That hand.'

She grinned. 'I could feel your territorial emanations from where you were standing.'

'She knew, too, didn't she? Ellie, I mean.'

'She certainly did.'

I stared at the two sketches again. 'If these affect him that way, God knows what a full-blown painting will do.'

Sue laughed out loud. Her cheeks were rosy. 'Dynamite. John Quinn said Lewis's painting was pure testosterone. And more explicit things. Think of that very phallic painting that belonged to Iris Barry: *The King and Queen in Bed*. Unless it's an abstract or war painting you come across, I think you've got a problem, Tim.'

I ignored her. Looking from one drawing to the other, the slight differences in handling were causing me to form an impression that somehow combined the sharper Nancy Cunard with the soft Alick Schepeler. As they overlapped, the face that assembled itself from the components was so familiar that I had to blink, squeeze my eyes together, and refocus in a deliberate attempt to blot it out.

'What's the matter?'

'Nothing. Come on, we should rejoin the throng. Jeremy will have arrived by now.'

'Not yet. You look pale. What is it?'

'Nothing. Maybe this room's a bit stuffy. I – I'm just a bit hot, that's all. Come on, let's go back to the others.'

She frowned, still watching me intently. 'Don't tell me you're getting hot flushes. What's up?'

It was ridiculous; how could you take a sharp angular face like Nancy Cunard's and combine it with Alick Schepeler's broader physiognomy to obtain a credible amalgam of the two? It was not just ridiculous, it was absurd. Yet the image persisted; high forehead, thick eyebrows, pronounced cheekbones, expressive, wide eyes, and a mouth – Good God –

'Tim! Sue! Piers said I'd find you in here admiring his Lewis etchings or whatever.' Jeremy White, leaning through the door-frame, grinned at us meaningfully. 'Don't leave us too long, or we'll think the worst.'

'Really, Jeremy.'

'Sorry, Sue.' He was not in the least contrite. His beam remained broad. 'Piers is absolutely delighted. Says you've agreed to take him to see the Wyndham Lewis when you find one. I told him he's highly honoured, providing he doesn't mind the danger. You've never done that for me, Tim.'

'Of course I have.'

'Never! Not at the start of the hunt. Anyway, I'm not jealous. I'm pleased that you and Piers seem to be getting along. There's a great deal to – but no, not at a party. Sorry, Sue; mustn't talk shop. I'll tell Tim tomorrow. Come on, both of you; lot of people to meet.'

He led us briskly away from the bedroom and back into the throng, which seemed to have intensified. I caught sight of Mary, Jeremy's wife, who's an old friend, and took Sue across to chat as I hurried to drop the disturbing image-portrait from my mind. After a while they were so deep into the White children's latest goings-on that I moved away and did my stuff by engaging various business acquaintances of Hargreaves's in rather useless banalities. I've never been convinced of the merits of that kind of contact and this assembly reinforced my prejudices. The face-image started to return as someone or other rattled on about the latest Lottery handouts. Ballet and opera are not my favourite pastimes either, but the plaint was so tired that my attention wandered; I listened to someone else on the subject of Clinton's presidency.

Time seemed to be going by. Unedifyingly.

Suddenly, I found a spectacled man, rather plump and featureless, with wispy hair, at my elbow. Beside him was a strong-faced woman, perhaps fortyish, dark, rather handsome in a powerful, dramatic way, with the prominent cheekbones of an actress.

'You're Tim Simpson, aren't you?' the man said, extending a freckled hand.

'Er, yes, I'm sorry –'

'Eric Waters, I'm with Medallion.'

'Oh! Sorry. I didn't know. But I've heard of you, from Charles Massenaux.'

He smiled. 'That's right. I hear you're an old friend of Mike Watson's, too.'

'Yes. We were at college together.'

'This is my wife, Sarah. Sarah, Tim Simpson, of White's Bank. The Art Fund man, amongst other things. He's on Piers's board.'

His wife smiled at me rather intensely and shook hands, but didn't say anything. Her eyes went over me appraisingly then flicked away to someone beside us who was laughing just a bit too loudly. The noise was starting to make it difficult to hear.

Behind his glasses, Waters's eyes were pale blue. 'Mike tells me that Charles Massenaux is probably going to be very good.'

'I'm sure he will.'

'We need it; Channel Three has started a rival programme to the BBC now. An antiques quiz.'

'Oh dear.'

Waters shrugged. 'It was bound to happen. We'll just have to be better. Piers is convinced about Charles Massenaux too, so we seem to stand a good chance. Mike Watson is one of our best.'

'Good.'

His wife Sarah was looking at me intently. When I caught her eye she smiled again, as though expecting me to address her about something specific.

'Have you known Piers long?' It was feeble, but as much as I wanted to manage at that moment.

'Oh yes.' Waters answered for both of them. 'Quite a long time. We were associated at Bergendale Press for a while.'

'I see.' Chummy, I thought, the way Piers and his contacts keep it all together.

'Piers is new to you, I suppose?'

'Yes.'

'How do you find him?'

'Er, well, he seems to be very pleasant. To me, anyway.'

The wife smiled meaningfully. 'Not quite the ogre you expected, then?'

'Oh, er, well, I wouldn't say I –'

Waters gave his wife a warning look, but she ignored him. The smile broadened into a meaning, theatrical one. 'You don't have to be shy. We all know Piers's reputation. A bastard by definition and a bastard to work with. Isn't that so?'

I felt slightly shocked. 'Er, well, I've no –'

'Didn't you know?' Her voice had acquired a metallic edge to it. She didn't seem to care who overheard. 'A lot of Piers's drive comes from the fact that he's illegitimate. In fact, most of it. His mother was called Hargreaves. She wasn't married; it's said that his father was a City man.'

'No. I didn't know.' I stared at her in genuine surprise. I was rapidly taking back what I'd been thinking to myself about cocktail parties as a source of information. None of the publicity about Hargreaves had ever mentioned his family details.

Waters cleared his throat. 'Yes, it's true. Not a public matter. Piers keeps it very secret.' He gave his wife another warning look, but it was too late. 'It's rumoured that his father was a man called Lamberville, who never acknowledged the paternity. You might recall, he was a sort of Charlie Clore in his day. Big shot. Had quite a lot of lady friends.'

'Oh. Yes, I do remember something.' An image of a tall, arrogant-looking man I'd seen in magazine-article photographs over the years came to me. 'It's before my time. Property, too, wasn't he?'

'In the good old days, yes. Hargreaves's mother was a secretary.'

'A bit like me,' his wife chipped in, with another meaningful smile. 'But I'm an amateur actress as well, aren't I, Eric?'

Waters frowned. It gave the weak face a distorted look. 'There is a sort of resemblance – to Lamberville, I mean – but it's not that evident. I hear he's very impressed with your Fund.'

'He's been complimentary, so far.'

'So much so that I gather you're going to include him in your next purchase excursion?'

I stared at him, very irritated. If it got round publicly that I was after a Wyndham Lewis, the whole exercise would be useless. Prices would be ridiculous.

My expression had Waters hastening to explain. 'I'm sorry; we were over by the passage. I couldn't help hearing what he said as he and Ellie came back into the room. He seemed to be very pleased.'

'Oh. Well, yes, in principle. But I have nothing particular in view just yet. We tend to be very confidential about our purchases. Until they are made.'

'Of course. Of course. I'm sure Piers is exactly the same. Don't worry; mum's the word.'

'Thanks.'

The bodies around us moved to allow the waiter through and as they moved I caught a glimpse of Sue. She was talking to Ellie Hargreaves rather animatedly and as she spoke, Piers Hargreaves came up to join them. He put his arm round Sue, not his wife, and I saw the material of Sue's dress crumple.

'Excuse me,' I said to Waters and his sharp lady.

I didn't move too quickly, so it took me about thirty long

seconds to get through the throng without knocking anyone over. By that time Hargreaves had removed his arm from Sue and put it round his wife's waist. All three of them stared at me as I reached them. There was an awkward moment's silence; I felt that Hargreaves had certainly seen me coming. 'Tim? How's your glass? Empty, I see.' He gesticulated and the waiter appeared from nowhere to take my empty glass and proffer another. 'Refill?'

I shook my head and the waiter withdrew. Somehow I believe I kept my expression neutral. 'No, thanks. I've enjoyed it, Piers, but I think we should be going.' I smiled at Ellie Hargreaves. 'Thank you very much. Especially for letting us into your bedroom to see the Lewis drawings.'

She looked surprised. 'Oh, you mustn't thank me. Thank Piers. They're his precious ladies. He says they keep him company when I'm away.'

He smiled modestly. 'That's true. My girlfriends, I call them. But you can see them whenever you want. Please feel free to come over any time. I've another one of Lewis's up at our place in Haddon; I'll save that for when you can come and visit us for the weekend.'

He made it clear that he was addressing us both.

'That would be nice,' Sue said.

She said it more to Ellie than to anyone else and it was a pretty standard sort of response, with no real commitment, but I still found I didn't like it. I held my hand out and shook both of the Hargreaveses' in farewell. I waved to Jeremy and Mary and then got us downstairs, into a taxi, with commendable speed.

'I'm so glad you didn't hit him,' Sue said, as we sat back and let the taxi motor to the west of Regent's Park.

'Sorry?'

'I thought you might. Your face as you came towards us was a picture for me. I'm not sure what they thought.'

'If he thinks he can start mauling you he's going to see the inside of a hospital.'

'He didn't maul me. He put his arm round me. It wasn't necessary, or particularly nice, because I happen to find I rather like Ellie and he's obviously trouble with women. But it doesn't do you any credit to behave like a threatened rhinoceros. Or me. These things happen at parties. You know they do. It doesn't mean anything.'

'It does to me. Especially after the bedroom episode.'

'Oh, that. Wait – now I think of it – what was wrong with you in there afterwards? Just before Jeremy came in?'

'I saw you. I saw why he's behaving towards you the way he is. The way he did in front of the drawings. It's not just party behaviour.'

'You saw me? You saw me what? What are you talking about?'

I bit my lip. 'The drawings. If you put Nancy Cunard and Alick Schepeler together, you get you.'

'*What*? What on earth are you saying?'

'Sounds absurd, doesn't it? I couldn't believe it, either. But if you half-close your eyes and look from one drawing to the other, you can sort of combine the faces. And the combination comes to you. No wonder he was behaving like that. Putting an arm round you was the last straw.'

'Tim! Are you ill? What on earth is the matter with you? It's crazy!'

'Piers Hargreaves obviously gets some kind of effect from those two drawings. All of a sudden he found he'd got the synthesis of them right in front of him. In his bedroom.'

'That's – that's absurd! Disgraceful! Mad! It's not true. Anyway, he's only just married Ellie.'

'So what?'

Suddenly, Sue started to laugh. 'You – you – Tim, I think things are affecting your – you need a doctor – some sort of help – you – I –'

She let her remarks trail away as she chuckled. Her eyes were wide and she sat round half-sideways to look at me and shook her head. The taxi pulled up outside Onslow Gardens. She got out first and was gone; by the time I'd paid the cabbie off she had let herself into the flat. I closed the door to find her staring at herself in the hall mirror. Her mouth was slightly open as she cocked her head from one side to the other.

'It's true, isn't it?'

She turned away from the mirror to stare at me with a revealing, puzzled frown. She didn't shake her head. I didn't have to say anything. Her mouth opened a little wider and her face was flushed. I took hold of her shoulders.

'No, Tim –'

But she didn't really mean no. When all is said and done about behaviour, although we are accused of this aggression and that, although some would demand permission to be obtained in triplicate beforehand or the proceedings to be expected to follow predictable routines, unresistible passion has no rules. It will not wait for courts to judge. Fear and anger, hope and certainty, unknown threats, flattery, lust; more than just the heart pounds when they take possession.

Sue's hesitation and resistance lasted mere seconds. Then she put her arms around me, tightly.

'Stupid boy,' she said.

14

I woke up to hear, far distant it seemed, the telephone ringing in the living room. I couldn't move. After a few moments I realized that Sue was lying half on top of me, one arm and one leg flung over, head under my chin, and that although we were decorously under the covers, we were otherwise completely naked.

The phone persisted. It wasn't even breakfast time yet.

'Don't answer it.' Her voice was muffled; hot breath warmed and moistened the side of my neck under my ear. There was thick, shiny, fragrant hair close to my mouth.

The phone wouldn't stop. I made a tentative movement of some sort but met with fleshy resistance, alternatively soft, alternatively firm.

'Leave it.'

This time her voice was not so close to my neck. Some pressure lightened somewhere but her movement and the closing of her hand in a proprietorial grasp were unambiguous.

I left the phone unanswered.

After quite a long time and much activity that I cannot describe, we sat at the breakfast table by the long windows, dressed back in everyday disguise, looking at each other, as people do on such occasions, and finding a great deal new to see. Sue's face seemed fuller than it does on normal mornings, with a tinge of puffy contentment that suited her. Her eyes were languorous in movement, slow and calm but watchful. They followed my every movement, stayed on my eyes for long periods, as mine did on hers, and both approved of what they saw.

We were going to be late for work.

The affirmation I had received from Sue, not just in the tumultuous passions of our return from St John's Wood but again that morning, had made up my mind. I decided that I would resign from Christerby's board. I did not need to belong, if the consideration of my views recently was anything to go by, and the Art Fund certainly did not need me to belong.

What I wanted was some distance between me and Piers Hargreaves. I wasn't frightened of him, I could deal with him if need be, but I felt he was malign. There was no need to subject Sue to the stresses that would arise if the association continued. I would keep my promise about the Wyndham Lewis when I heard from Mr Brooks again. If I heard from Mr Brooks again. But Hargreaves was a tempest best avoided until it blew itself out. Jeremy would bluster but I'd made up my mind about that.

Altogether it was a bad time for the bank. And for me, except in my marriage.

I looked yet again across the breakfast table. 'Sue, I've made a decision. I – '

The telephone interrupted, making me curse. Sue's slight frown was followed by a quizzical smile as I got up reluctantly to answer. That wretched instrument is so difficult to deny; breakfast intruded upon again.

'Tim?'

'Richard?'

I had no difficulty in recognizing the voice. Sir Richard White, immured in his Dordogne *bastide anglaise*, has often been my director in the past.

'I'm sorry I probably disturbed you earlier. I forgot that your clocks went back last weekend and we are once again an hour ahead of you, not the same time.'

'That's right.'

'My sincere apologies to you and to your dear wife if I abbreviated her beauty sleep.'

'I'll pass them on. But I am certain she'll forgive you.'

'How kind. Are you both well?'

'Fine, thanks. And you?'

'Well, thank you. You've read the papers this morning, presumably?'

'Er, no, Richard, I haven't had the chance so far.'

'In that case, I will enlighten you. Bergendale Press has gone into receivership.'

'Oh? Oh. I see.'

'Do you? I am sure that with your usual discernment you will have identified the strategy Hargreaves is intending. He hinted very broadly at it during the last board meeting of Christerby's, according to Hamish, who spoke to me afterwards. I do not have to tell you that I do not approve. What do you think?'

'I – I'm not sure that I agree with this so-called communications and education strategy, Richard.'

'Good. I'm glad. It is a basis for nakedly ambitious empire-building, of course. The concept that Christerby's would profit from owning their own catalogue-printing facilities is ridiculous. Hamish says that he introduced you to Hargreaves. What did you think?'

I hesitated for a moment. I knew what I thought but how could I express it? 'He's going out of his way to be pleasant to me. We were at a cocktail party of his last night.'

'Ah. Indeed. Well, that fits with what I am about to tell you. But what is your opinion?'

'I'm afraid I don't trust him. For both personal and professional reasons. I also believe that he is nakedly ambitious. But he is currying favour with me and Jeremy in a way that is difficult to reject. He has pleaded to come with me when I next go to buy something for the Art Fund. He's a Wyndham Lewis fan, you see.'

'Wyndham Lewis? You're going to buy a Wyndham Lewis?'

'If a good one can be found, yes.'

'Very perceptive of you, Tim. That may help you in what I have to say. This morning, when you get to your office, Jeremy will ask you to abandon whatever projects you are currently handling and proceed to Bergendale Press in Northampton.'

'What?'

'Your reputation as a troubleshooter and business consultant is very high. Especially on past form. Hargreaves has suggested, indeed pressed Jeremy most insistently, that you should be seconded, in view of the bank's interest, to do a quick assessment of Bergendale Press before an offer is made by Christerby's to the receiver.'

'To buy Bergendale Press?'

'Exactly.'

'But that's appalling! Hargreaves himself was an expensive board member there not so long ago. It was he who buggered the whole place up. He knows better than anyone what state it's in; it's his doing. Now he wants to snap it up cheap; it's disgraceful. He doesn't need anyone, let alone me, to do an assessment.'

'Precisely. But there you have the subtlety of the thing. By getting an "up-to-date" assessment by White's themselves he can show the necessary objectivity. He can claim that Bergendale did not follow his advice and that he is now the white knight – oh, pardon the pun – who will rescue it from closure, using Christerby's backed by White's Bank. Once this objective is achieved he will proceed to the next step towards his ultimate plan, which is, of course, to get a seat on the main board of the bank.'

'*What*?'

'I perceive you are as horrified as I am at the prospect. He must be stopped at all costs. That is why I need you urgently to accept this commission. Knowing you as I do, my immediate reaction was that you would indignantly refuse it. But you must not. I need you, Tim, to be on site and well informed so that this dreadful creature can be dealt with. Faithfully.'

'Does Jeremy –?'

'Your loyalty to Jeremy has always been faultless. But Jeremy is distracted by the problems of merchant banking in this frightful decade. He thinks that projects like Hargreaves's may provide the answer. There are other aspects, too. Hargreaves has made enormous efforts to seduce Jeremy. I am glad that you remain unimpressed. You will, as I say, be asked to join in this charade this morning.'

'But I – I –'

'I would take it as a personal favour if you would stifle your natural reaction and accept the Bergendale Press investigation. Hargreaves must be stopped. The web of associations he intends – between Bergendale for print, Wappinger's for software and hardware, and Medallion TV – a communications empire – will lead to disaster. He, however, will undoubtedly profit. He must be stopped. Will you accept the commission?'

'With reluctance, Richard. But in view of the way you ask, of course.'

'Thank you, Tim. I shall not forget this.' There was a pause, then, before I could chip in, he asked: 'You said, by the way, that your objection to Hargreaves was personal as well as professional. Was that just natural antipathy?'

'Richard, I think I should tell you that last night it became obvious that he is taking an unhealthy interest in Sue. His request for me to be seconded to the Bergendale affair – and occupied in Northampton – may be motivated in part by that interest. More than part.'

There was a moment's shocked silence. 'But the man has just recently remarried.'

'Nonetheless. I won't take up your time with the evidence and the circumstances, but it is so, obviously, to us both.'

'In that case' – the voice had suddenly gone richly humorous – 'although I must deplore the repugnance your dear wife must feel – her taste has always been impeccable – you will forgive me if I rejoice.'

'Rejoice? Why?'

'Because it means that unless he abandons his interest, which on past form he is chronically unable to do, he is a doomed man.'

'That bad, am I?'

'To your eternal credit, yes. But if you wish to withdraw, I will understand.'

'Oh, no. A promise is a promise. And now that I've woken up to the circumstances, especially the danger to the bank, it will give me great pleasure.'

'Thank you, Tim. I'll be in touch.'

'Richard.'

He put the phone down. I turned to look at Sue.

'Richard has asked me to accept a consultancy project at Bergendale Press which Hargreaves has asked Jeremy to second me to. I would have rejected it. I was going to resign from Christerby's board so that we wouldn't be troubled by Hargreaves. I was about to tell you when the phone rang. But Richard has asked me to continue as a personal favour.'

She got up from the table and came to stand in front of me. 'Resign? Run away? That doesn't sound like you.'

'I – I didn't want you to be subjected to – to Hargreaves. Richard says your taste is far too good, though.'

She put her arms round me carefully and squeezed just gently. 'You wouldn't protect me by running away, would you? But I can deal with my side of things. You don't really have any doubts, do you?'

'Well, no, but –'

'But what? Do you really think I resemble a combination of an alcoholic nymphomaniac and an artists' model-cum-secretary?'

'Of course not! They're just drawings.'

'Well, then. What's your problem?'

'I didn't say I thought you'd fall for his vulpine charms. I wanted to protect you from something unpleasant.'

'Tim, Tim, you are so dense sometimes. Promise me just one thing.'

'What?'

'Don't go killing Piers Hargreaves, will you? You'd be no good to me in gaol.'

15

'And so, you see,' Jeremy White said to me across his large mahogany partners' desk, a desk he had insisted upon despite the fact that there would never be a partner to sit on the opposite side, 'it is vital, absolutely vital, that you get up to Bergendale's as soon as possible. Both in your role as a board member, a director of Christerby's – '

'A non-executive director, Jeremy.'

'Yes, yes, yes, don't start labouring that point. Non-executive directors have a role, indeed are expected to contribute, positively contribute, to the firm of which they are a part, no matter how, er, how – '

'Peripheral?'

'No, no, not peripheral, you know exactly what I mean. Stop interrupting. Both, as I was saying, as a director of Christerby's and as a member of the bank's highly esteemed investigative staff. Your reputation on previous assignments has assured the board, the main board that is, that the very highest quality assessment will be made.'

'How kind, Jeremy.'

'Look here, it's only a week ago you were complaining that you weren't being consulted properly about things at Christerby's. You can't object now that we're asking you to get stuck into this most important project.'

'Potential project, Jeremy.'

'Yes, yes, yes, if you must be pedantic. Potential project then. So what's wrong?'

'Nothing that I can think of, Jeremy.'

'What?'

'I said nothing that I can think of, Jeremy.'

'What? You mean that you'll do it?'

'I did say yes, Jeremy, a few moments ago. But you were too far gone, in full spate, to hear what I said.'

He goggled at me incredulously. 'You – you agree?'

'Yes, Jeremy.'

'You'll drop everything else? I mean, you'll have to get going right away, you know.'

'This will have absolute priority, Jeremy.'

A look of deep suspicion came into his face. 'Including the Wyndham Lewis?'

'But of course, Jeremy. Paintings must take their proper place behind real business. My apologies will have to be conveyed to Piers Hargreaves. In view of his interest in this Bergendale affair, however –'

'Interest? Interest? For God's sake, Tim, it's the man's most passionately felt project! He specifically asked for you to be put on it! The Wyndham Lewis is nothing. A mere – a mere –'

'Bagatelle?'

'Diversion! It must be dropped until this matter is concluded.'

'When you say concluded, Jeremy, do I detect a certain predisposition towards the outcome?'

'Of course not.' His head reared up. 'There can be no question that the terms, conditions and situation must be properly considered. The board will not entertain the financing of anything without the strong probability of a successful outcome.'

'Ah. Good.'

'The current situation is too serious for anything else. But we cannot shrink from real life. Our heads must not go into the sand. The communications highway is – is –'

Bullshit, I nearly said. But it would not have been tactful or clever at that moment. My cards had to remain close to my chest.

'– one of the most exciting future industries in which to be involved.'

For a moment I really felt quite guilty. I have worked for and with Jeremy for a long time; he is a quite superlative man in many ways, with all the canine qualities, and we have been through a great deal together. His enthusiasms, however, have always required a certain reserve before execution. When in the mood, he sparks off ideas like a catherine wheel and that simile does not occur just because we were then approaching November the Fifth. Jeremy and I make a good team; we balance each other very well. Neither of us is ever absolutely right but together we do get results. There are many successes that would not have occurred if Jeremy had not initiated them. On the other hand, it has never paid to tell Jeremy everything at once.

'I'm – I'm very glad that you are taking a positive attitude towards this, Tim.'

'We mustn't get stuck in a rut, Jeremy.'

'Absolutely not! It'll mean that you might have to be away for a few nights though, mightn't you? Do you think?'

'It's possible. But Northampton is hardly very far off. It's not that one can't get there within an hour or two, depending on the traffic.'

'Oh, absolutely. But knowing your, er, inquisitive nature and the need for speed, you might be late, or might do some scouting, reconnaissance as it were, further afield?'

'I'll have to play that by ear, Jeremy.'

'Of course. Well, mustn't keep you any longer, then.'

'Indeed not.'

'You'll get the details of the receiver and everything? It's a local firm's appointee.'

'I will.'

As I got up to leave, I felt another pang. His face was a picture: surprise, even astonishment, mingled with pleasure and suspicion, makes up an entertaining mask. For the viewer. But then I reflected that he and the board had inflicted Piers Hargreaves on me and everyone else without any consideration for our feelings. The thought suppressed any desire to come clean.

I went back to my office to clear my desk and was greeted by a rather inquisitive Penny, notebook in hand. I looked at her appreciatively but with caution. Penny is a fair, wide-hipped girl with brisk, supervisory manners retained from her time as a prefect at her public school. There is nothing spinsterish about Penny; despite her high standards of selection, she has many admirers, one or two of whom can be taken seriously. But it is a part of her character to want to know everything, despite its irrelevance to her work or personal life.

'You're off to Northampton, I gather,' she said.

'Yes, Penny. I am impressed how quickly the office grapevine still works.'

She smiled smugly. 'Will it be for long? I heard not.'

'In that case, it will not be for long.'

'A few days?'

'At the most. You can get me on my mobile phone any time.'

'Will you be staying up there? Do you want me to book an hotel?'

'No, thanks. But you'd better call the receiver – Jeremy's got the details – and make an appointment for me pretty quick.'

She waited for a moment to see if I would volunteer any opinion on the outcome of my visit, so that she could relay that on to the secretaries' network too, but got nothing, so looked down at her pad.

'There was a call from a Mr Macdonald.'

'Ah. At last. What did he say?'

'He sounded very cautious.' She frowned at the memory. 'He was extremely cryptic. He said to convey Mr Brooks's sincere apologies for letting you down and that he'd be in touch again, very shortly. Said you'd know what it was about.' She looked at me curiously, and waited.

'Thank you, Penny. Anything else?'

A slight frown came to her face. 'A Mrs Waters phoned. She was very cryptic, too.'

'Mrs Waters?'

'Yes. Rather a – a fruity-voiced woman.'

'Mmm. And what was her message?'

'She wouldn't leave one. Said she'd phone you back.'

'Fine.'

Her face, like Jeremy's, was now a picture, but a different one. I wasn't pleasing Penny at all. Not even a reproof for her disrespectful description of the voice, which might have been a friend's, but then the reproof would have provided identification.

'Then Charles Massenaux phoned. Can you phone him back urgently?'

'Ah. Of course. I'll do that right away.'

'He's not in Bond Street. It's a mobile number. He's at Milton Keynes.'

'Milton Keynes?'

'Yes. He's out with this TV programme they're making.'

'In Milton Keynes? Good God. Poor Charles.'

She pursed her lips and handed me a sheet from her pad. I waited until she left the room, then dialled.

'Charles?'

'Tim. Hang on – this is a mobile phone. I'm moving to somewhere discreet.'

'How is art life in the new towns?'

He didn't hear me. When he came back on the line he sounded quite cheerful. 'I'm glad you called back. We had rather a good session yesterday evening; quite interesting, really. You'd be amazed what comes up.'

'Good. How's Mike Watson doing?'

'Oh, he's a tremendous fellow, Tim. Great chap. We get on really well. My goodness, he's told a few stories about you at college that have had the crew's hair standing on end. They all want you to come on the set when we get back. To meet you.'

'Thanks. I'll forego the pleasure.'

'Oh, don't be like that. My God, though, I thought I'd heard it all but I've never heard the one about you and the fandango with Maisie Buggins in the Bombay Tandoori after the Steele-Bodger match.'

'Did you phone me to gossip about revelations on my salad days or was there something you really wanted?'

'Tim, Tim. Don't get narked; I only wanted to repay a debt.'

'Oh?'

'Yes. One good turn deserves another. I'm very grateful to you, dear boy, for your intervention at the dress rehearsal.

It made all the difference. So despite a possible conflict of interest, but in view of your help and my attitude to Hargreaves, I'm going to give you a lead I should be following up.'

'What's that?'

'Last night we were open to a public audience. After the show – I ran through quite a lot of interesting gear – a very rural old dear came up to me and asked if there could be any interest in what she called a horrible big painting her husband whitewashed over.'

'Charles –'

'Wait for it, dear boy. Wait for it. Get a pencil and paper ready. She said that it was sort of all squiggles and things. An abstract, obviously. It was so big they lent it to a local amateur dramatic society, who used it as part of a backdrop for their Christmas show. That's when they whitewashed it. Her husband put it back in a barn afterwards. He died ten years ago. The barn's used by her son – they're small farmers near Paulerspury – and he wants to clear it out along with a load of rubbish so as to store barley straw or something. It sounded dreadful and I was about to say no when I thought about the squiggles and things. I asked if it was Cubist, but of course she didn't know. But she did say something when I asked her if it was signed. She said she thought it was but her husband painted it all over and it's so dirty now, you can't see. But she thought it might be a name that sounded something like Lewis.'

'Charles, there are several other Lewises, you know. Quite apart from Bert Lewis, the famous farming painter from Paulerspury.'

'Tim, where's your old enthusiasm? I'd go and look myself but we're moving on to Chester tomorrow. Quite apart from the danger.'

'What danger?'

'If you're looking for a Lewis, there'll be danger. Don't be so ungrateful. And so stick-in-the-mud. Here, write it down.'

He gave me an address in Paulerspury, talking about directions from Pury End or Plumpton End or somewhere like that, and I wrote it down.

'Will you go?'

'As it happens, Charles, I have to go to Northampton over the Bergendale thing.'

'What Bergendale thing?'

'Not on the phone, Charles. I'll tell you when you get back. What do you think of show biz? A life on the open road?'

'Actually, we've had quite a bit of fun. The first show goes out in two days' time. Have a look and see what you think.'

'I will. Happy landings, then, Charles.'

'Don't let the old biddy down, will you? I said that I had a colleague who'd be along very quickly.'

'Thanks.'

'Ungrateful swine. I should go myself but you know how it is: the roar of the greasepaint, the smell of the crowd. See you soon.'

'See you.'

The line went dead. I looked at the address. It was only then that it occurred to me that the place was just south of Towcester, on the old A5 Watling Street, near where an old dealer I once knew told his story about the big Malta painting by the side of the main road. That came from a farm barn near Towcester, too.

Where fat George Welling said he came from.

Prickles started down my spine. But just then Penny came back in with the name of the receiver at Bergendale, confirming an appointment that very afternoon. There was no time to lose if I didn't want the whole of White's Bank down on my neck. First things first: I shoved the address into my pocket and went off to find my car.

16

The receiver at Bergendale Press was a short, dark, cheerful man called Plackett, with the businesslike demeanour of an undertaker briskly ordering up the next load of coffins. Like an incoming cuckoo, he had taken over the company secretary's office, an old-fashioned room panelled in the manner of thirties walnut and still occupied by a large, grey, gloomy safe, with a brass handle on the front door the size of the locking lever on a submarine bulkhead.

'It's no good sizing that up,' he said, catching my glance towards the ponderous, castored steel box as I was ushered in, 'there's not a brass farthing in there.'

I grinned as I shook hands with him. 'Not even the deeds to the old home?'

'Not a hope.' Plackett was an accountant with a local Northampton firm who were said to be doing quite well out of the recession. 'The property was all mortgaged to the bank a long time ago. This has been on the cards for ages, I'm afraid.' A look of genuine regret crossed his face. 'It's getting to be quite depressing how so many of what seemed to be the better firms are going under. We've been used to the shoe trade taking a pasting, but now it's quite a few of the newer technologies that can't seem to keep up. Still' – realizing he had a profession to perform and a sale to make, he rallied himself – 'as a going concern, this firm has some very good prospects for the right buyer.'

'You think so?'

'Oh yes.' He waved me to a chair in front of a dappled burr-walnut desk piled high with files and papers. 'Did you have a good drive up?'

'No problems, apart from one set of roadworks.'

'Good. I could have sent you the papers but I'm sure you're right to have a look for yourself. Tea or coffee?'

'Tea would be fine.'

'Milk and sugar?'

'Thanks.'

'It's a machine down the passage, but it's not too bad. Excuse me a sec.'

He bustled off out of the office door and I took a slow look round. Whoever the company secretary had been, he – it wasn't a woman's room – hadn't done much to alleviate its feeling of depression. There was a rubber plant. There was a framed certificate from the Institute of Chartered Secretaries and another from the Institute of Chartered Accountants, one hung above the other. Otherwise the art works displayed were an aerial photograph of the works, black and white, about ten years old, and two or three mass photographs of staff – about sixty or seventy of them – on some sort of outings or official anniversaries. I guessed that Plackett was right; Bergendale had been on the down slope for a long time. Nothing in the office told of cheerful prosperity. I got up to peer at one of the mass photographs just as Plackett came bustling back, wincing at the heat from the plastic cups of scalding tea he held in his hands. I relieved him of one of them and sat down again.

'Cheerful snaps, aren't they?' Plackett waved at the walls. 'About half that lot got the chop a year or so ago. That's when the incumbent of this office topped himself.'

'Dreadful. I heard he jumped off the roof or something?'

'No, no. The papers got it all wrong. That was a different matter. An accident with a roofing contractor. Everyone said it was a bad omen. The company secretary and chief accountant – Parsons, he was called – hanged himself from an apple tree at home. His wife went into the garden to do some weeding one afternoon and there he was, dangling from a big sour Bramley. Gave her quite a turn. He couldn't face it, you see. He was the one who would have had to hand out the notices and pay the men off.'

'Poor devil.'

'Yes. As it was, one of the other directors had to do it. Nasty job, especially as he'd been given the push himself. It was a traumatic clearout. Anyway, I've got some figures together for you. Here, take a look at this lot.'

He handed me a large sheet of figures and I began to take them in steadily. It wasn't very difficult to get a grip on the facts from the balance sheet. The firm had owned the premises but these were all mortgaged to their bank. There was some quite good equipment: two big four-colour Heidelbergs, a two-colour Roland, and quite a lot of computerized origination and art-work stuff.

'Who owns the machines?' I asked.

Plackett pointed at the lower part of his sheet. 'It's leased. London firm called St Pierre Leasing. Part of a big finance group.'

'So the assets are negligible.'

'Oh, well, I wouldn't say that. And there's a good backlog of orders, really. Tremendous goodwill, you know. The expertise here is first rate. No union problems. I've managed to get agreement from all the suppliers to carry on, on a pro forma basis, of course. Paper's the big item; prices have gone through the roof this year.'

'That's what's put the final boot in, hasn't it?'

He pulled a face. 'I suppose you could say that. But if, as I understand it, your firm puts all its colour catalogue work over here, you must have a going concern.'

He was talking to me as a director of Christerby's, even though he knew of the bank's involvement. I kept my face deadpan.

'Is absolutely all the equipment leased?'

'Yes. You'd have no trouble taking it over, though.'

'I don't know this firm – St Pierre Leasing – I'll get the details from you and contact them.'

He looked at me wonderingly. 'I thought it was your boss who introduced them?'

'My boss – oh, Piers Hargreaves. Did he?'

'That's what I've been told. When he was here before the big massacre. Got good terms from them or something. They seem pretty standard to me – the terms, I mean. That's the information I've been given, anyway. Bit brief, the survivors here are. Your man's not the most popular figure, I'm afraid.'

'I can imagine.'

He gave me a long look. 'Have you worked with him for long?'

'No. First time I've come across him. He was appointed while – while I was out of the country. I'm a non-executive director of Christerby's. My real job is at the bank. Hargreaves is a new appointment.'

'Ah. Well, enough said.' He got up briskly. 'If you've done with your tea, I'll show you round the works and you can meet the people. I'm afraid most of them are pretty shell-shocked.'

A couple of hours or so later I was back in my car, sitting in the chill autumn dark, thinking: this is stupid, I didn't need to come here for very long. This is a credibility job. Oh yes, I can hear Hargreaves saying, Tim went up there and thoroughly cased the place; we've done a searching analysis. What the hell was he up to? Pure empire-building? Did he really foul this business up so that he could engineer a cheap purchase later on? Was he as Machiavellian as that?

I've never much believed in the Fiendish Plot theory; the Cock-up is what my experience has mostly found to be the case.

And if Hargreaves thought that by handing me this little job he'd get me out of the way for some sort of attempt on Sue, he was badly mistaken. There was no need for me to stay away from home over this simple caper.

I looked at my watch. Just gone six. I dialled up the office but Penny and Geoffrey had both gone to a City reception connected with a foreign bank's exchange department. That meant nothing by way of information until tomorrow. I put the phone down and took Charles Massenaux's crumpled address paper out of my pocket. Paulerspury; not very far away. Why not? My promises to Jeremy wouldn't be broken if I just checked; it was ninety-nine per cent certain that the lead would come to nothing, anyway.

I telephoned the number on the note and an old crone answered, her voice rising with pleasure when I explained

125

about Charles's message. Yes, she said, I could come right away. Her son was working outside but she'd tell him I was coming. She gave me directions on how to get there.

I drove out of Northampton, past the motorway crossing and down the A43 to Towcester, turning off at the town southwards to join the old A5, the Roman Watling Street.

Never ignore a call on that bit of Watling Street.

Down the long, straight, undulating stretch to Stony Stratford, in the old days before the motorway was built, this was a main route from south to north. Near Potterspury, there was an antique dealer who had a business in an old stone house that was reputed to have been an inn who told me about a huge, dirty marine and harbour battle painting he bought out of a nearby farm, a canvas so big and so difficult commercially – battle scenes weren't popular then – that he propped it up against the wall out on the road for the heavy passing traffic to see, as a sort of advertisement hoarding. At the end of a long day, and some sporadic rain, a foreign dealer with a shipper's runner drove in and bought the painting, all splashed with mud, for a couple of hundred quid, quite a decent price in those days. He forgot all about it until, a year later, the foreign dealer returned, driving a new Mercedes. It turned out the painting was an early period representation of the Siege of Malta and the foreigner, a Maltese, sold it to a Valetta museum for a fortune. God only knew how it had got to the farm; the dealer said it must have been stolen so long ago there was no problem of title to it.

So you never can tell what'll turn up on the old Watling Street; I crossed my fingers as I drove.

The farm was well off the road, down a longish single-width lane with a good bit of stone wall about. My Jaguar XJS started to feel a bit wide, but I supposed that farm implements had to come down there, so pressed on. Eventually I came across a group of stone buildings that corresponded with the instructions, and drew up in a floodlit yard.

A big, overalled, booted muddy fellow in his fifties came out of a side door as I got out into the chill damp air and nodded affably enough to me as he approached.

'Mr Simpson?'

126

'Yes.'

He extended a broad hand. 'Jim Merrick. My mother said you'd be along. It's good of you to come. She's quite excited – she goes to this antiques circle locally and they did an outing to Milton Keynes, to see your colleague, you see, that's how it all came up. I don't think you'll be impressed, though. I've wanted to chuck the ruddy thing out for some time. It's been in the barn for so long and it's too big for any normal house, so I thought no one'd want it. My father painted it all over with whitewash, then the panto people – well, we may as well go and look at it right away. Get it over with. It's a bit short notice, so I haven't had time to get the junk round it cleared, but I think you'll be able to see enough. Do you mind meeting my mother afterwards? She sets such store by this kind of thing.'

'I'd be glad to. I've got a torch if – '

'Oh, no. There's a light in the barn and I've got a lamp on a cable.' He grinned. 'All mod cons here, you know, even if farming is at the end of its tether.'

We crossed the yard to a large stone building, me dodging the mud, and he pulled open a small door set in the huge wooden ones made of battered planking that closed off the main entrance. Inside, as he switched on a rather dim, high central light, my nostrils hit the smell of mingled hay, straw, manure, oil, paraffin, creosote, grain and damp, dirty stone walling typical of working agricultural buildings; a good, honest, working smell that can't be faked. We went under a mezzanine floor supported by beams and he switched on a light under the decking so that we could thread our way past some spiky machinery covered half in rust and half in mud.

'Back here,' he said, and pulled out a caged light bulb in a socket on the end of a long black rubber lead. 'Mind your trousers – there's some sharp edges about as well as mucky ones.'

At the end of the section the back wall was piled with hurdles, a tubular metal gate and various planked doors. Behind them were some high poles, like hop poles, stacked almost vertically so that they took all the weight of the accumulated hurdles and gates leaning against them.

'There you are,' he said, pushing a door to one side and moving the lamp closer to the back wall. 'It's a big thing, ain't it? I aim to clear out this whole area soon and get some straw in. I can't even get at the stud wall behind until this lot's moved.'

I blinked in the alternating bright light and shadow. Outlined on the wall was a huge dirty grey canvas with what looked like a tree and a house crudely painted on it.

'My father lent it to the local am-drams,' Jim Merrick said. 'He whitewashed it over originally – bit grey now, ain't it? – and they painted that tree and house on in emulsion. They needed some backdrops for *Jack and the Beanstalk*. I thought it was terrific – the panto, I mean, not the backdrops. I must have been about twelve, so that tells you how long it's been like that. The stage seemed enormous – it was the village hall – and that was only one of the screens they used, but it can't have been that big, not now that I think of it.'

I squinted at it, past the bright caged bulb. 'Any idea what the size is? It looks more than six feet high.'

'Seven.' His voice was confident. 'I can tell you it's seven feet because those poles are eight and they clear it nicely enough to lean on the stud wall and stop this lot pressing on the screen. Beg pardon, canvas.'

A slight shiver went through me. Seven feet high; absolutely dead right, according to one of the books.

'How long d'you think? About, what, eight feet or so?'

'Longer.' He gestured forward. 'That hurdle there's eight. hang on: I've got a tape in me pocket. Here, if you don't mind holding the light, I'll be able to get it more accurately for you. Is it important?'

'Could be.'

I took the light and he rummaged in his pocket to produce a steel, coiled builder's measuring tape. After a lot of heaving on hurdles and moving of gates, he managed to take, at a short distance, enough spreads of the tape to satisfy himself and turn back to me.

'Nine feet,' he said. 'Any good?'

I must have shivered visibly.

'Getting cold o' nights now,' Merrick nodded. 'But it stays pretty dry in here.'

It wasn't what he thought. When John Quinn's collection was sold up in New York in 1927, an ex-friend of Lewis's called Dick Wyndham, no relation, who he had parodied in *The Apes of God* along with the Sitwells, bought a whole heap of Lewises for almost nothing. Among them was *Kermesse*, said to be nine feet by seven.

'I'll relieve you of the lamp.'

I handed it back to him. 'Your mother told Charles – that's my colleague – that she thought there was a signature under that lot. Lewis?'

He smiled tolerantly. 'There might have been. Hard to say. It's been covered for so long. I'll have to tell you that her memory's not what it was. By no means. I don't remember a signature. It was such a jumble of splashes and spots and strokes of paint; that's all I remember of it. Ugly thing, I thought. But you never can tell these days, can you? I saw a thing called *Weeping Woman* by Picasso in a magazine t'other day. Horrible, it was. They said it's worth a fortune. But then no one used it for the panto, did they?'

I smiled. 'I don't think so.'

'Can you get that lot off, d'you think? The emulsion and the whitewash?'

'Oh yes. But it'd cost a lot to do it properly. If there's reason to believe there's a good painting underneath you don't just take a load of hot water and a scrubbing brush to it. Or the turps bottle.'

He chuckled. 'I should think not.'

'I think I've seen enough. Can we talk to your mother now?'

'Of course.'

Dick Wyndham, who was a sort of dilettante artist himself, advertised two paintings for sale in *The Times*, in September, 1930. One was nine feet by seven, the other six by four. He asked for twenty and fifteen pounds each respectively. A few shillings per square foot, he told his friends, that's all that

Wyndham Lewis paintings are worth. God knows what Lewis said or thought.

No one knows what happened to them. Not up to now, anyway.

Mrs Merrick was a small, bright-eyed, ancient country-woman, rather brown in colour, with grey hair pulled back over her head. In the kitchen with her was her daughter-in-law, an ample woman in her fifties, like her husband. They both beamed at me expectantly and wouldn't be satisfied until I'd sat down at the table and accepted a large mug of stewed farm tea.

'He says it'd cost a lot to take the whitewash off, Mother,' her son advised, once we'd both taken a draught.

'But is it worth it, Mr Simpson?' she asked.

I hesitated for a moment before replying. 'It's an unusual size, Mrs Merrick. We could clean off just around where the signature should be, if there is one. Then if it's the right signature it'd be worth going on. But even the first clean should be done by a professional. Can you please try to remember the name on it? My colleague Charles Massenaux said you thought it was Lewis.'

Her brow clouded slightly. 'I'm fairly sure it was Lewis. I can't be so sure now. It's been so long since my husband helped the panto out. Forty years or more.'

'You never took a photograph of it?'

She shook her head. 'No.'

'You don't remember where your husband got it?'

'Oh, yes. He was a great auction-goer. Mostly for agricultural things, of course. Stock for the farm. He bought it for three pounds, more as a joke than anything else, but because he was always a magpie, way back in the fifties at Colville's. There was an old house in Stony Stratford they were selling up and the contents came to their yard here.'

'Who did you say? Colville's?'

'That was the local auctioneers. Agricultural, mainly. They became Ross and Colville in the seventies, before they went out of business.'

The prickles returned and I had to suppress a shiver whilst keeping my voice normal. 'Good heavens. You don't by any

130

chance know of a George Welling, who used to be with them until recently?'

All three of them smiled but it was Jim Merrick who answered. 'Fat George Welling? Good Lord, I haven't heard of him for ten years – that's how long it is since Ross and Colville went out of business, not recently. Bunter Welling, we used to call him at school.'

'You were at school with him?'

'Sure I was.'

'Isn't he an antiques and art consultant now?'

This time their smiles turned to laughs. 'Bunter Welling? He wouldn't know an antique from a goose. Farm stock, that's what he dealt with. How do you come to know him?'

'I – I heard of him through a friend. He hasn't contacted you recently?'

'Good heavens, no. What reason would he have to do that?'

'Er, none at all, I suppose. Just wondered.'

'Well, he hasn't been in the auction game for at least ten years, to my knowledge. When Colville's closed he got a job over Northampton way, on the road as a firm's rep or something.'

'From what I heard' – Jim Merrick's wife looked thoughtful as she spoke – 'he went to live over the other side of Northampton. In Wellingborough, I think.' She stopped, then her face cleared. 'No: Wilby, that was it. Just outside Wellingborough.'

'Would that be in the local phone book? I'd like to call him. On – on behalf of this friend, who's lost contact.'

'I think so. I'll have a look for you.' The daughter-in-law got up and disappeared further into the house.

Jim Merrick gave me a long, cool, farmer's look. 'If this painting is by Lewis, and it's the right Lewis, what'd it be worth?'

'Quite a lot. You'll ask what's quite a lot. I don't want to excite you without foundation, but if it's a Wyndham Lewis, in my estimation, somewhere between fifty and a hundred thousand pounds.'

His jaw dropped open. His mother stared at me, her gaze transfixed.

I spoke carefully; you have to be circumspect in possibilities like this. 'I am saying that it might be worth nothing. But I'll tell you what I'm prepared to do. I'll arrange for the painting to be moved to a good firm of restorers. I'll pay for them to take off some of the overpaint and see if they can find a signature. In return, I'll ask you to sign an agreement that you'll give our Art Fund first option to buy it if we want to. Otherwise it will cost you nothing.'

Jim Merrick stuck out his hand. 'Agreed.'

His mother bridled. 'It's my painting, Jim. I haven't given it to you yet, have I?' Then she smiled and turned to me. 'But I'll agree to that, too. Then I will be able to give it to Jim and Dorothy so they can get the farm back on a decent financial basis again, won't I?'

'If you're going to do that, you'd better say you gave it to them ten years ago. Then there won't be any transfer tax problems – if it turns out to be valuable.'

'Oh, Mr Simpson, I can see we're going to need your advice.' She smiled at me brightly and I winced, thinking how unlikely it all was. Yet you never knew, the description, the size, no amateur's size; it could be, it was worth a try.

Jim Merrick's wife came back in, shaking her head. 'I'm sorry, but there's no George Welling in this one. Yet I'm sure he was in the book once. This is brand new, mark you.' She turned to her husband. 'Jim, isn't there an old one in the barn office? By the Amstrad?'

He nodded. 'Almost bound to be. Haven't thrown it away. I'll go and look.'

'If it's any trouble,' I said, 'please don't bother.'

'It's no bother. You've done us a good turn, maybe. Least we can do.'

He was back five minutes later with an address in Great Doddington, near Wilby, outside Wellingborough.

'That's just over a year ago,' he said. 'At least you might be able to trace him from that.'

'I'm very grateful.'

I finished my tea, thanked them, and left. George Welling

would have to wait until tomorrow, but my mind was working overtime as I drove south.

The question I was asking myself was: what kind of rep, or art and antiques consultant, has no phone?

Answer, maybe: one who hires a studio by the week. And whose colleagues get knocked down by cars just outside Oadby, which is not so very far – about thirty miles – north of the Merricks' farm.

17

I knew something was wrong as soon as I walked in the door. It was after nine, I'd had a long day, and Sue was sitting in front of the fireplace, on the settee, staring at me, knees together, the way women do when they want you to know that no, it's not all right and although you're home you can't relax, there's a crisis.

'What's up?' I asked.

'Someone has been photographing me,' she said. Her eyes were round and her face was taut.

'What?'

'When I came out this morning and went to the car, I saw him.'

Sue has been known to walk to the Tate from Onslow Gardens in good weather but normally she drives her little MG Metro to the gallery, where she has a place in the much-coveted car park.

I sat down next to her on the settee. 'Saw who?'

'The man. He was sitting in a car not far away, just across the road, and he had a camera. He sort of put it down and almost hid it when I looked towards him. I didn't think much of it, then. He was an ordinary-looking sort in a windcheater and I thought perhaps he was taking shots of the Gardens or something, not that they're much of a sight just now. But then, when I came out after work, I saw him again.'

'At the gallery?'

'Outside. It was the same man in the same car. And he still had his camera out.'

I frowned. 'Surely it must have been getting dark?'

'It was. Almost. That's why it was so odd. I left early to

134

get home in good time so there was still some light, but not a lot.'

'Did he know you'd seen him?'

'I think so.' She stared at me. 'Our eyes practically met.'

'Did you recognize him? I mean, have you seen him before?'

'No. He's no one I know. That's what's even worse, in a way. I mean, why? Tim, what do you think it's about?'

I shook my head. 'I've no idea.'

'Honestly? Really, truly, honestly?'

'Honestly. I'm not involved with anything that –'

'What?'

The thought had occurred to me about images of Sue's face and who might want them.

'Tim?'

'Maybe he was just photographing pretty girls,' I said, lamely.

'And following them to the Tate? And waiting there all day? There's lots of pretty girls to photograph everywhere and I'm not one of them. You swear none of your Wyndham Lewis contacts are in this?'

'What on earth for? Why would they want to photograph you?'

'I – I don't know.'

'Have you had anything to eat? Have you had a drink?'

She shook her head. I got up, poured her a sherry, did the same with a whisky for myself and sat back next to her.

She took a sip then looked straight at me. 'You think it's Piers Hargreaves, don't you?'

'Yes. I'm afraid I do.'

'Why?'

'Who else do we know of, recently, who would want to get images of you? Who else would hire a man to do it for him? To collect the pictures at a distance, so to speak?'

'He – he can't really be like that, can he? It's terrifying. Obsessives like that are horrendous. I don't want to believe it's him. If it is, what on earth will we do?'

'Let's not jump to conclusions. It may be completely

135

unconnected. Mistaken identity, even. You didn't get the car number, by any chance?'

She smiled for the first time. 'I'm not your wife for nothing. Of course I did. It was a dark-blue Ford Mondeo.'

'Oh, well done! Don't worry, then; we'll get to the bottom of this. We mustn't prejudice the issue; there may be some simple explanation. Or we can quickly put a stop to it. I'll phone Nobby in the morning first thing and get him to trace the car.'

'I've already given the number to Gillian.'

Punctured, I had to smile. Chief Inspector Nobby Roberts is an old friend, an ex-rugger team-mate from college. His wife Gillian and Sue get on like a house on fire. Nobby wouldn't stand a chance of refusing to trace that number if Gillian gave him the job to do. Ignore the female network at your peril.

'What did you tell her?'

'Exactly what I've told you. Only I didn't say who I thought it might be. I – I didn't like to think while I was talking to her. I've thought a lot since. I was rather hoping, stupid as it may seem, that you might have had some sinister figure from your painting search that would explain it. The alternative is too awful to think about. Gillian said she'd give the number to Nobby as soon as he got home.'

'In that case,' I said, 'there is nothing more that can be done tonight. It only remains for me to get us something to eat.'

Which is what I did, however disturbed I was by the thought that Sue had been alone in that flat for at least three hours without thinking of food or drink. Her call to Gillian would have relieved some of the tension but she didn't relax very much, even after something to eat. She watched the television with sightless eyes while I assured her I'd accompany her in the morning and we went to bed fairly early, holding each other but full of unspoken thoughts.

In the morning, there was no car outside with any photographer in it. I escorted Sue to her Metro and, at a discreet distance, followed her to the Tate Gallery. There was no dark-blue Ford Mondeo with the number Sue had observed anywhere in sight. Nor was there any other suspicious car with a camera-equipped driver about. I saw her carefully into work and drove on to the bank, where I parked and was soon on the phone to Nobby Roberts at Scotland Yard.

He was his usual suspicious self. 'What have you been up to?' he demanded.

'Nobby, you must not always assume guilt on my part. This is an inexplicable matter. But Sue is pretty upset. How quickly can you trace that number?'

'Good heavens,' he said, 'with Gillian and Sue after me? I've traced it already.'

'My God, that's quick. So?'

'It's a hire car.'

'Oh, Jesus.'

'Have no fear. I'll have a man go round and start tracking down the company's records today. It may take a little time. Be patient.'

'Gosh, thanks, Nobby. You're a pal.'

Irony came into his voice. 'All part of the service. Anything more you want, just ring.'

I put the phone down and dialled Robert the restorer. Robert the restorer runs a very good picture-restoring business in North London and has every facility necessary. He employs three men and two girls and is extremely discreet, which is why I use him for the Art Fund. I told him about the big canvas at the Merricks' farm and he said they had a pantechnicon coming down from the Midlands which would pick it up that very morning.

'Good grief!' I said. 'That's quick. How will you do that?'

'Tim,' he said, with a tired patience, 'we have mobile phones these days, you know? Even our lorry driver. What is this enormous painting?'

I explained the condition to him and he chuckled. 'That's a new one. A panto screen? What do you think it really is?'

'Let us not prejudge the issue. We must be objective.'

'Oh, come on, give us a clue.'

I thought. I didn't want him to get excited, or to see things that weren't there. 'Try an Anglo-American connotation,' I said. 'I'm not going to tell you any more.'

'Meanie. I look forward to seeing this. Knowing you, there'll be a surprise.'

'Let's hope it isn't a nasty one.'

After that I thought for a moment, then went into Geoffrey Price's office. He was behind his desk, neat and tidy and morning-crisp, as an accountant should be, especially an accountant with four children and a Rover car, living in Hampstead and playing cricket on Sundays, though not at this time of year, when he hibernates in front of the TV at weekends, never missing Rugby Special on Sunday afternoon.

'My goodness,' he said. 'I thought you were up in Northampton.'

'I was. But I needed some information, so I came to see you. The oracle. The fount of all City finance knowledge.'

'Flattery only makes me suspicious. Especially from you. Does Jeremy know you're here?'

'I have no doubt that the grapevine is reporting to him right now. What I need, however, is your full works on St Pierre Leasing and Investments.'

He frowned. Something about him stiffened. 'Have you cleared this with Jeremy?'

'I beg your pardon?'

'Have you cleared this with Jeremy? The circulation is strictly limited. I have to have authority in writing.'

'Eh? Are we on different networks here or something, Geoffrey? I'm just asking if you have some information on St Pierre Investments?'

'And I'm saying yes, I have. But you can't have it. Not without proper authorization.'

Prickles were starting down my back all over again. I did my best to suppress them. I like Geoffrey. There is no call for me to get aggressive with him. But there are limits.

'Have you joined the Foreign Office or something? Need a memo in triplicate, do you?'

'No, not a memo in triplicate. Just a proper clearance.'

I gaped at him. There he was, the Geoffrey I have known for years, sitting behind his desk, smart as paint, talking sheer drivel.

'Clearance? What is this? MI5?'

'Tim, there are days when I think too many scrums have blunted your brain. The front row, with all that head-butting, is not best for enhancement of the little grey cells, I know that, but up to now I thought you'd avoided the worst damage. Perhaps it's delayed action.'

'Geoffrey, do you like hospital food?'

'For God's sake, man, I can't give you the St Pierre report because it's strictly limited to main board members, and not all of them; only about three. What is the matter with you?'

'The St Pierre report? You mean you have a St Pierre report?'

'Of course I have. You surely knew – oh, no. Oh, no.' He closed his eyes. 'You didn't, did you? You didn't know there was one?'

'No, Geoffrey, I didn't.' I sat down carefully, opposite him. 'Perhaps you had better tell me all about it, had you?'

'Oh, Jesus, I've blown it. How did you –?' He groaned. 'Oh, dear. It's existence is top secret, Tim. For God's sake, I can't give it to you. Not unless Jeremy instructs me to.'

'Why didn't I know about this?'

'Presumably because one, you've been away eating snails in garlic washed down by chateau-bottled claret, and two, Jeremy didn't want you to.'

'Very reassuring. All this happened while the loathsome Hargreaves was being appointed, I suppose?'

'Mmm, same sort of time, yes.'

'And let me get this straight: you have, here in this very building, if not right here in this office, a report on St Pierre Investments but you're not going to let me have it?'

'*Rem acu tetigisti*, as I believe the Romans put it.'

'This is incredible. That means I have to go to Companies House and dig the whole thing up for myself? When most of it is already here.'

'Why on earth are you interested in St Pierre? I mean, it seems extraordinary to me; you get sent to Northampton and within hours you are back here trying to jam your spoke into the wrong wheel. You can't be left on your own.'

'The wrong wheel? Bergendale's machinery is in thrall to

these faceless St Pierres – they might even be Frogs or something – so when I ask a perfectly civil question, as part of a perfectly logical process, you as good as tell me to find a barrel with a hole in it and get knotted. I've had enough of this; this is sheer obstruction.'

'It's no good getting snotty with me.' He waved a hand. 'Jeremy's just down the passage. Go and head-butt him. Stick your thumb in his eye, not mine.'

'Thanks, I will. Now.'

And I surged off down the passage. But Jeremy wasn't there, of course. He'd gone to a meeting. His secretary wouldn't say where; she said he'd be back tomorrow. He'd left strict instructions not to be contacted.

I glared at her but she didn't flinch. 'Bloody hell!' I said. 'Bloody, bloody hell!'

Penny came into Jeremy's secretary's office as I said it.

'Aren't you supposed to be in Northampton?' she asked.

'I am,' I growled. 'This is just a chimera you see here. A stupid mirage.'

Within minutes I was back in my car. I was spitting by the time I'd cleared London. I went up the M1 motorway like a dose of salts. I was boiling. I turned off before Northampton and headed for Wellingborough. Just outside the town, at the straggle of houses at Wilby, along the main A510, I stopped and asked for Great Doddington. A local pointed patiently at a signpost that said Great Doddington. I drove down that road. Topping a ridge that overlooked the watery sources and tributaries of the river Nene in the valley below, I came to a row of brick bungalows of pre-war design, some of them with neat gardens fronting the road. I stopped the Jaguar outside a less repainted, dowdy example and strode up to ring the bell. A rather timid old josser in a woolly waistcoat, brown trousers and carpet slippers opened the door a crack. I beamed at him cheerfully.

'I'm sorry to disturb you,' I said. 'I'm looking for George Welling. Do you by any chance have a forwarding address for him?'

The old josser's rheumy eyes went past me to the Jaguar. His face slackened slightly. 'You a friend of his?'

140

'Oh, yes,' I lied brightly. 'My name's Tim. Tim Simpson. Lost contact with him, I'm afraid.'

'From Bergendale's?'

I stiffened slightly. This was all getting a bit incestuous. Welling? Bergendale's?

The old man was waiting.

'In a way, yes. Connected with that.'

The door opened another half-inch. 'He still lives here.'

'Oh? I checked the telephone book but he's not in it.'

'No; it's in our name now. Halford. He lodges here. We agreed to let him have a room when we bought the place. It was a mortgage sale. Repossession, you know. He was out of work, like, and having a lodger helps with the expenses. Oh, Lawd: you're not from the DSS, are you?'

'No,' I said, wondering how many DSS inspectors have XJS Jaguars, and then thinking probably quite a few, 'I'm not from the DSS. Or the Inland Revenue. Is he in?'

The old man shook his head. 'Out. Went for a walk, yesterday. Not back yet.'

'Walk? Yesterday? Where to?'

A jerk of the head this time. 'I thought he went down the side there. Goes into the fields. Path all the way to Wilby. Past the orchard.'

'Orchard?'

'Yeah. Got some nice old English trees there. Don't like all those French Golden Delicious myself.'

'But yesterday?'

'Yeah. I don't tell him how long to be, do I? Big boy now, ain't he? Often away for more than a day, lately-like.'

'Excuse me,' I said.

I strode down past his bungalow, along the track his head-jerk had indicated. Don't ask me why. It was the idea of the orchard that disturbed me. The talk of sour Bramleys from Plackett. It was autumn but the leaves had stayed on the trees much longer than usual because of warm weather and the foliage was still quite dense. The old josser was right about the varieties; they were big, old, neglected trees, not the grubbed-up dwarf modern things that produce today's supermarket blandness.

141

It was a small orchard to the side of the track, with a tumbledown wall round it, relict of some earlier enclosure. I took a look out across the empty fields, over towards the distant water meadows cut by stream tributaries of the Nene, and turned off into the close. A few withered apples still clung unpicked to gnarled, knotty branches. I had to duck under unpruned, sagging, twiggy lengths. When I straightened, I was in the middle of the copse, where overgrowth had brought branches from different trees to overlap and interfere with each other, tangling thickly even higher up –

That was when I saw him.

I leant against a nearby trunk and put my head down. The feeling of giddiness faded after about thirty seconds. I took two deep breaths and made the effort to look up again.

He was quite high up. For a fat man he'd gone to a lot of effort, clambering up the sloping main trunk and throwing the rope over a thick outspreading branch before securing it to himself and then stepping or slipping off, so that he swung well clear for his neck to –

Afterwards, I wondered why he hadn't done it the easy way, with a length of rubber hose and the car exhaust. It's a much calmer way to go, gassing yourself quietly to sleep.

They said he couldn't do that because he didn't have a car. He lost it when Bergendale's made him redundant.

18

You might think, considering how uneventful is the life of an English policeman, that the man who presents them with a dead body would merit a little appreciation, even a touch of the old bonhomie, for enlivening the deadly daily routine of speeding fines and domestic argy-bargy with something more dramatic. One does not expect the admiring glance, but a bit of the yes, sir, really, sir, it was a remarkable find of yours, sir, must have given you quite a nasty turn that, come on, Sergeant, bring a nice pot of tea and some fairy cakes for the gentleman, is an approach that would go down quite well.

It's not like that at all.

Excited they are, with a suitably grave and serious demeanour, and all attention they are, and brisk and efficient and all that they are, producing carloads of men in overalls and rubber boots and an ambulance and all sorts of vehicles which apparently had nothing else to do but wait for the odd dangling corpse to turn up in an orchard, but their attitude to me was not quite what I might have expected.

Once they'd established that I'd got over the shock, and that I didn't need counselling, whatever that may be, for trauma or whatever, and that I was quite happy to give them a brief factual statement at the local nick and sign it, the local constabulary got into a sort of iffy, sniffy, suspicious mode. What exactly was my relationship with the deceased, they wanted to know. Business? What sort of business would that be? Then, seeing from my expression that whatever business it was, it was none of theirs, they explained that they were just trying to establish the deceased's background, you see, sir, and perhaps find out why he might have taken this dreadful step, if indeed it proved that he did take it himself and that there were no suspicious circumstances, which it didn't look as though there were, but you never could tell what forensic might come up with, could you?

It's just for the coroner, you know, they said, pencils poised, looking hopefully at me with the looks of policemen who have not made a decent arrest since the mayor was apprehended urinating against the public horse trough and drinking fountain after the last Masonic do.

There really are grave disadvantages to living in a country with one of the lowest murder rates in the world and one of them is that the force, admirable though it may be, has an unhealthy passion – rather like Penny's – for wanting to know the minutiae of things which should not concern them. In New York, I imagine they'd simply say oh yeah, another homicide or a suicide or one of those, check it out, Charlie, and go on about their business of testing car sirens or chewing gum, but here the rozzers are like the next door's mother-in-law, really they are.

I had two choices: I could either tell them that the last time I'd seen the deceased was in a studio in Notting Hill, with three other men, and that I'd bought a Wyndham Lewis drawing of Iris Barry, the model for *Praxitella* (could you just spell that for us, sir?), for two thousand five hundred pounds off him and his mates, and then found out that the studio didn't belong to any of them, but the one who'd rented it gave a false address, and possibly name, to the estate agent from whom they took it and subsequently one of them was squashed by a car coming back from a pub on the Oadby road or, and this was the 'or' I chose, I could tell them that I was doing a very confidential investigation for the bank into the possible purchase of Bergendale Press as a going concern and that I had wanted to speak to George Welling as one of its ex-employees on the sales side.

Their eyes widened at that. They rather liked that. There was, in addition to the clandestine nature of my assignment and the unusual thoroughness of my approach, a rather graphic social and moral tale to tell about the dreadful effects of redundancy and middle-management or sales-force rejection caused by the government's economic policies, not to mention the same's interference in police-force organization with a view to cruel cuts in funding. They wrote that down with convinced satisfaction. They nodded with massive approval when I gave them the receiver, Plackett's, name, in case they needed a reference whilst emphasizing that I expected absolute secrecy. I had to appreciate, of course, that they were Wellingborough men and that Northampton, which must be at least seven miles from where the incident occurred, was not in their jurisdiction, but they'd heard of Plackett's firm. Local verification of this sort proved to be quite sufficient; I was allowed to leave, even escorted to my car, with a deal more respect.

They said they'd be in touch if necessary.

I felt a bit guilty, really, about withholding the Notting Hill end of things but I'd lost a lot of time already and Jeremy would go bananas if he thought I'd been wasting my efforts on the Wyndham Lewis affair instead of Bergendale's. But now the two had crossed over; I didn't like that, not at all. That was too much to be coincidence; life doesn't do that, or at least it shouldn't, even though you read of such chances in the newspapers over and over again.

I decided to go back to Bergendale's. I didn't feel sure of myself at all, now. I didn't know what the hell was going on and clearly it was up to me to find out by myself. No one was going to help me; I was the mug, the potential scapegoat in all this. And although I felt it was a waste of time to go round Bergendale's again, talking to whoever would talk to me, there was a routine to go through, a decent thing to do, decent by the remaining employees and decent by the standards of the bank. I mustn't let those decencies pass by.

Plackett wasn't at all surprised to see me. People imagine that purchases of firms require a lot more fieldwork than they really do. In reality such purchases are more usually the work of accountants, poring through figures, than real people looking at real objects and getting reactions from the world out there. I told Plackett I needed to look through some more figures, especially the sales ledger, and he nodded in understanding. I spent what remained of the day, which wasn't much, looking through the figures. I wanted to talk to the sales manager, too, but they said he'd gone up to Manchester to try and land some orders and wouldn't be back for two days. It turned out that he was new, anyway; the last sales manager got the chop at the time of the big clearout, when George Welling got his.

I took another look at the dismal staff photograph and sure enough, there was George Welling, fat as ever but smiling then, that happy day when they all stood for the works photograph and no one was thinking about getting the chop. I hate photographs like that, after the event.

I left relatively early – just after five – because I didn't want Sue to be on her own for long. I phoned home and she was there already; she sounded calm and said she was OK; there was no photographer anywhere, maybe it was all a mistake, she was going to make me some supper, when would I be back?

I gave her an anticipated time and set off. They were just starting a new set of roadworks south of Newport Pagnell and, seeing the lorry putting cones down, I realized I was lucky to miss a bad blockage. They never can leave the old M1 alone; later, that would be important.

It was halfway down the Finchley Road that my mobile phone rang. Robert the restorer came on the line.

'Tim? Your office gave me this number. Hope you don't mind?'

A frisson went through me. 'Robert? I don't mind at all. You're working late.'

'A man's work is never done. It's about this big number we picked up for you this morning.'

'What's up?'

'I was curious. You know me. I had a wipe at it about an hour or two back and I've stayed on a bit to make sure.'

'Already? You haven't wasted any time.'

'Yeah. Well. Some of it came off quite easily, actually. The whitewash part, I mean. You're a cunning devil, but you can't fool me, Tim. I've dealt with one of these before. A Yankee job, it was, for one of the big oil men.'

I was stationary at the Swiss Cottage lights. Rain had started to fall and the windscreen became spotted. 'Oh? Come on, Robert, spit it out. I'm all agog.'

'Splots and splashes; I don't have to tell you who that is.'

'It's not a Wyndham Lewis?'

'Nah. 'Course not. Come on, Tim, don't let me have to spell it out for you. You've landed a right big fish here, you old fox. How did you do it?'

The traffic was moving off. I went with it, but slowly, making someone hoot at me from behind. In a minute, I'd have to turn the wipers on; the drops were starting to run into little trickles.

'It's abstract?'

'Sure.'

'Is it signed?'

'Possibly. I can't be too sure, but I'm pretty certain it will be. It's unmistakable. Come on, Tim: splots and splashes. Big Yankee.'

I stared at the dappled windscreen, all spots and trickles running into each other, as what he was saying sunk in and the breathtaking thought dawned.

'Oh, my God! Oh, no. Not a Jackson Pollock?'

'You're a cunning old devil, you are, Tim; you knew all the time, didn't you?'

19

'A corpse and a Jackson Pollock.' From behind his big desk, Jeremy's face was a picture as he struggled to control his emotions whilst going into a ferocious, declamatory declension. 'I do not want a corpse. I do not want a Jackson Pollock. We do not want a Jackson Pollock. The Fund does not want a Jackson Pollock. No one in his right *mind* wants a Jackson Pollock. American art museums *might* want a Jackson Pollock. But we have gained nothing. Absolutely nothing. Christerby's New York will most probably reap a rich harvest. We, on the other hand, have simply lost time. Valuable time.'

Geoffrey Price was listening, entranced, from my side of the table. His jaw was slightly open and his eyes observed Jeremy in silent delight. It seemed it was up to me to say something.

'Um, that's not quite true, Jeremy.'

He glared at me. His eyes were quite pink. Just down the passage, his secretary and Penny would be huddled rapturously together, ears straining. In fury, his voice rose to accommodate them. 'You specifically promised, you gave me your solemn word, that you would not divert from the project with which I have entrusted you to go sidetracking off on diversions of this sort.'

'That is not quite true either, Jeremy. I said that Bergendale would have absolute priority. I assure you it has.'

'I was encouraged to think that you were seeing sense. I was quite heartened at what seemed to be your agreement to cooperate. I was wrong. I should have known your capacity for deception. I am sadly disappointed. Not only have you, in what I can only call the most classic, the most characteristic fashion, discovered a body hanging from a large pear or an apple tree – '

'Blenheim Orange, actually. Unusual, that – '

'Don't interrupt! Do not interrupt me! Not only, as I say, have you confirmed my worst possible fears by adding to your lamentable record, your predilection for *stumbling upon*, as you so blandly put it, yet another corpse' – he actually clutched momentarily at his head with both hands – *'yet another corpse*, my God, when will it end, *when will it end*? – you openly admit that, in addition to wandering off all over the countryside into body-strewn orchards when you should be pursuing my specific, my precisely defined instructions, you have also been rootling about in random barns in order to come up with not even the wretched Wyndham Lewis you were seeking but one of the worst possible examples of what I think is called Abstract Expressionism. In huge, unmanageable form.'

'Pollock always painted big, Jeremy.'

'Tim! Don't – '

'And this seems to be an example of his finest period, the so-called "drip" period. Before that, in the words of one writer I vividly recall – '

'Tim! I'm warning you – '

'– Pollock explored the terrain of the prelogical but excluded bizarre Surrealist fantasy and literary symbolism.'

'If you don't – '

'Vaguely totemic images, often suggestive of ritual, served as points of departure for authentic experiences. During the 1948 to 1950 "drip" period, however – '

'That's it! That's it! Shut up! Just shut up!'

'Jeremy, you must control yourself. You'll have a heart attack if you go on like this.'

'I'll have a heart attack if I don't do something about you! Now!'

It was time to stop baiting him. 'I have not lost a single minute on the Bergendale affair. I have, despite the brutal obstruction of my own colleagues, pursued all the necessary avenues of assessment – '

'Stop! Stop right there! What the hell do you mean: "the brutal obstruction of your own colleagues"?'

I gestured towards Geoffrey Price. 'I have asked Geoffrey to join us this morning to confirm that despite my formal, reasonable and, I might add, perfectly polite request, I have been refused access to vital information already existing in this building. Information which would have assisted and speeded me in my assessment.'

He blinked. 'What information?'

'Information on the St Pierre investment group.'

His whole frame congealed. It was worth a pint or two just to watch his change of expression. From rank fury his face contorted into shock, incredulity and even fear, in that order. What remained was deep suspicion.

'What the blazes do you want that for?'

'They seem to have more than a passing interest in this matter.'

'That's quite irrelevant! A simple leasing contract for the printing presses does not justify your wasting time prying into the parent company structure, for heaven's sake. You must concentrate on the matter in hand. Something you seem to have become incapable of doing. You're always going off at a tangent.'

I leant back in my repro-Chippendale chair, put my hands behind my head and eyed him narrowly. 'How did you know that St Pierre was the machine leaser?'

He was still on the defensive. 'I – I – I can't remember. Not that it is of any importance. My source is of no importance at all. The important thing is to have your report, without delay, to put in front of the main board. Who are anxiously awaiting it. Why is it too much to ask you to *get on* with doing what you're told?'

'I am getting on, Jeremy. A few mere minutes, when the works was closed anyway, have not delayed anything you need.'

'If someone else pips us at the post and snaps up Bergendale from under our noses, I cannot protect you, Tim. Indeed, I shall not protect you.'

'Oh, I shouldn't worry, Jeremy' I said, drily. 'No one is going to pip us at the post.'

'Why not?'

'Snap up Bergendale? A demoralized printing business with mortgaged assets and departing customers? Despite what the receiver says I've checked their client list. It'll soon be down to nothing. The sales manager is up in Manchester desperately trying to whip up trade. The only argument for Bergendale's survival is if some outfit with a big four-colour print order comes out of the blue, and you know who the only likely one of those is.'

'You don't know that! You don't know, either, if another printer might want all those facilities.'

'Jeremy, have you looked at the print trade magazines lately? There are pages, not just one or two, but pages of Heidelberg and Roland presses for sale, four-colour, reconditioned, ready to install. Machinery dealers would fall on your neck for an order. They're having to knock most of them out for export. If Bergendale go under, the leasing company will be left with a load of scrap iron on their hands.'

That silenced him for quite a few seconds. I kept my hands behind my head and viewed him sardonically during the break before speaking again. 'That hush-hush, is it, Jeremy?'

'What?'

'Whatever it is that's going on with St Pierre Investments.'

'I – I am sworn to secrecy.'

'So we're not going to be told whether they are buying us out or we them.'

He licked his lips. 'In today's City climate it is vital that absolute secrecy is maintained. Rumours could be very damaging. For that reason, the numbers involved in the – the matters we are examining must be kept to an absolute minimum. That way, if a leak takes place, we'll know where it was sprung. Let me assure you, Tim, that we are looking at several things and there have been approaches from several directions. They all have to be dealt with very carefully.'

His voice had a crushed element to it, an element I hated to hear. I put my hands back down. I felt a bit guilty. Jeremy was fighting desperately, if I knew him, for the survival of

151

his family's business, a business he was as proud of as the poor bastards up at Bergendale had presumably been of theirs. The odds were against us. If you'd asked me to bet, and I'm not a betting man, cold reasoning would have me lay money on White's not existing within the next year. Like Kleinwort Benson, if we were to survive, current trends would have us belonging very soon to some foreign outfit, wanting a foothold in Europe's leading financial market. The thought was hateful to Jeremy. It's all very well saying, as so often it is the wise thing to say, 'take the money and run,' or, 'always sell on a rising market,' but if you keep on doing that what's left of you in the end? Who are you? A rich retiree or someone else's lackey, that's who. If Jeremy needed any help to prevent takeover he could rely on me, whatever fracture that might cause with the main board, from whom, clearly, he was under dreadful pressure.

'Jeremy,' I said, 'I must apologize if I've caused you upset at a time when you have more important things to deal with. You'll have the report very quickly. I promise you no one else would do it quicker.'

His eyes met mine. 'Thank you, Tim. I accept. And you have mine if I became too intemperate. We had all better get on with our work. I take it these people at the farm are pretty delighted?'

'Oh yes. And so are the restorers. They say that distinguishing the original splattered Jackson Pollock from the panto overpaint will keep them occupied for quite a long time. Charles is as pleased as a dog with two whatsits. He's assured the Merricks that when the thing is put up for sale in New York it'll fetch big money.' I sighed. 'All in all, it's good news for everyone. Except us. It's not often that you go out to look for a Lewis and come back with a corpse in an apple tree and a Jackson Pollock, overpainted for the village panto.'

It was then that Geoffrey Price couldn't help it. He looked at me, shaking his head from side to side, and started to chuckle. As he chuckled, even Jeremy started a smile and then, as they both burst into merriment, I had to get up and go to the door to look down at them, looking back at me and rocking with laughter at the sight.

Tears began to run down their faces. Jeremy got out a white handkerchief and began to dab with it.

'Pollocks to both of you,' I said.

And left.

20

Nobby Roberts took a sip of his beer, picked up a knife, looked with approval at the composition of the ploughman's lunch in front of him, especially the moist slab of Stilton cheese, put the pint of bitter down, picked up a roll of crusty bread and looked at me keenly from under his ginger eyebrows.

'Is there anything you'd like to tell me?' he asked.

That's typical of policemen, that; you lure them along to a gash lunch on the promise that they are going to divulge a vital bit of nerve-racking info to you and they start by asking questions. I frowned back at him.

'I thought that you were going to cough up the goods to me, Nobby,' I countered.

Nobby smiled faintly. Nobby is a lean, tall, fit sort of bloke who played on the wing in our college rugger side when I was in the scrum. He was very, very good and I thought he should have got his blue, but there were too many good wings about just then and not enough front-row sloggers, so I got a blue and he didn't. He is a dedicated, very professional and moral sort of policeman, with a genuine vocation towards society. He views my career with considerable scepticism. One of the ironic things about Nobby and me, I often think, is the way in which our roles have been reversed. At college he was the fleeting skirmisher on the wing while I was the plodding, muddied oaf of the grinding front row. Now he is the solid, dependable citizen, although perhaps not so plodding, and I have become part of society's outriders, the wheeling predators who pick off the financial fruits so briefly to be snatched when the eye spots the passing chance.

154

Nobby does not approve of merchant banking; Nobby does not much approve of the art trade either, having been a member of the Art Fraud Squad during part of his sojourn at Scotland Yard.

On two counts, therefore, I do not impress Nobby.

He applied knife to a pat of butter. 'The man who hired the Ford Mondeo,' he said, 'of the number Sue gave to Gillian, was a Swiss.'

'A Swiss?'

Nobby nodded emphatically. 'A Swiss. He provided his driving licence, which had an address in Zürich on it, and also his passport. The hire-car company were perfectly correct in their procedures.'

'But – but – a Swiss?'

'Name of Müller. Not very original, but apparently true. He returned the car to Heathrow within thirty-six hours as agreed in the hire contract. And presumably toddled off back home.'

'Good God! What on earth was a Swiss called Müller doing, taking shots of Sue?'

Nobby did not reply at once. He spread the butter on to the piece of crusty roll, cut a slice of cheese, put it on the roll, added a bit of pickle and bit into the combination with a look of anticipated satisfaction. 'Not bad Stilton, this,' he mumbled through the wad.

'Can anything be done to find out?'

He gave me a look as he chomped to reduce the mass in his mouth. 'I have faxed the Zürich authorities to let me have any information they have on this Müller, including anything about him that may be relevant. Switzerland, however, is not part of the European Union. The Swiss police tend to be very guarded about their citizens and I shall almost certainly receive back a long form asking me to reconfirm in more detail for what purpose this information is required.'

'That's typical.'

'It is in the interest of the private citizen that his or her personal interests and private affairs should be safeguarded from unwarranted intrusion.'

'In Switzerland? The most nosy society in Europe? And

155

you can talk; you lot, in that Lubianka on Broadway, have the goods on so many private citizens it's a wonder any of us are allowed to walk free at all.'

'We do not have such goods, as you call them. There are many occasions on which I only wish we had.'

'There you are, then. An absolute blank. Müller has vanished back to Zürich with photos of Sue, taken for reasons that we may never know.'

'I'm afraid that may be the outcome, Tim. How is Sue taking it?'

'She's calmed down a bit since it happened. Especially as it seems to have been a one-off. She's still pretty jumpy, though.'

'I am afraid there is nothing to prevent people from taking such photos, provided they do not breach certain regulations and their execution does not constitute an assault or definite harassment. Our society is very open in that way. Tourists-tout photographers, for example, used to snap your image in the street and attempt to sell you the result. You don't see so many of those now; private cameras have mostly put them out of business. But within certain constraints it's not illegal, providing they don't obstruct the pavement.'

'I don't understand it.'

'All is not lost. The Swiss authorities in question owe me a favour, actually. We do collaborate quite smoothly, you know. Give it a day or two and something may come up.'

'It's baffling.'

'That's what Sue said to Gillian this morning when she told her the news so far. Although Gillie had the impression Sue was holding back a bit on something. You know how women are; intuition and all that.'

'Um, yes.'

He looked at me levelly over a raised glass. 'So there isn't anything you'd like to tell me, is there?'

I suppose that interviewing criminals in back rooms of police stations leads the Nobbies of this world to persist in this fashion. I frowned at him again and said, 'You asked me that before.'

'Indeed I did. In my long and painful experience, you see,

apparently inexplicable events connected with you are often to be explained by your activities, associations and general lack of restraint in so-called business affairs, often conducted with the criminal element in our society.'

I knew he'd be both personal and remorseless; there's no getting round him once his curiosity is roused. 'Nobby, between you and me there is a new MD at Christerby's called Piers Hargreaves who I think may be taking more than a passing interest in Sue. An unhealthy one.'

He blinked. 'To the extent of hiring a Zürich photographer to take snaps of her in the street?'

'I – I must admit it sounds far-fetched. But he's a bit strange. Very strange, in fact.'

'I've heard of Piers Hargreaves. I suppose a lot of people have. Tell me: what form does his strangeness take?'

In as few words as possible I described the scene in the Hargreaveses' bedroom. Nobby frowned. 'It's hardly the basis for bringing a man, at considerable expense, over from Zürich for the purpose of obtaining images of Sue to compare with two drawings which you, in what might be the heightened atmosphere of a party, think combine to give a likeness of her, is it?'

'It – it sounds ridiculous, I agree. But Hargreaves is the only candidate I can think of. He's got that sort of obsessive-possessive behaviour pattern. The potential megalomaniac, I mean.'

'Oh, Tim. Now I'd say you've been reading too much psychoanalytical stuff. Or watching *Cracker* on television.'

'Nobby, if you read back through his divorce cases I'm sure you'll find a pattern of behaviour that includes a sort of reverse persecution mania. As I recall, he set private detectives after the wives and had them photographed in all sorts of places.'

'Collecting evidence for grounds for divorce is not quite the same thing as what you're suggesting, Tim. I'm devil's-advocating your suggestions, not necessarily saying they're wrong, you understand.'

I fell silent. I couldn't remember the exact detail, but something I hadn't told Sue stuck in my mind about the newspaper reports of the Hargreaves divorces, something about private eyes and street photographs. I'd have to look it up.

'Is that the only theory you have?' Nobby asked.

'At the moment, yes.'

'Oh.' He was getting to the end of his cheese. 'I'm disappointed. I thought perhaps you might have another theory.'

'Another theory?'

'Yes.'

'I – I'm not sure what you're getting at, Nobby.'

'Aren't you?' He smiled, one of his really unpleasant, interview-back-room smiles I recognized immediately, one that over the years must have made many an offender quake in his boots without the tape recorder getting a squeak on it. 'You do surprise me, Tim.'

'Surprise you? Why?'

He sighed. 'It is, happily, a feature of modern policing that computerized records have speeded up procedures. Not to the extent that you implied just now – we have yet to get identity cards introduced in Britain, whereas many of our Continental colleagues have that advantage – but we're not doing too badly.'

'Aren't you really? Bully for you.'

'Sarcasm ill suits you, Tim.' His smile became more penetrating. 'I had a call yesterday. From the Northamptonshire Police. The detective sergeant in question is handling a case of apparent suicide at a site near Wellingborough where, it seems, a redundant salesman hanged himself from an apple tree. Although foul play was not, initially, suspected, it seems now that the forensic team have expressed some doubts about the ability of the man to hang himself in the way that he did. So the sergeant, with commendable efficiency, decided to check into the known facts.'

'Nobby, I –'

He held up a commanding hand. 'Wait. Wait for it. The detective sergeant examined the testimony of those interviewed about the dead man – his landlord, his ex-employers, etc., etc., and, not surprisingly, the person who found the body. One Simpson, Timothy, of that ilk. And the sergeant, being an efficient and thorough policeman, checked the name of Simpson, Timothy, in the computer records and hey presto, guess what the computer records said?'

'And you claim,' I said bitterly, 'that this isn't a police state?'

'The records said that in the event of this man's involvement it is recommended that a check be made with DCI Roberts, at Scotland Yard. So that is what he did. Amazing, isn't it?'

I had a flashback of Mr Brooks's voice, on the telephone, ranting on about surveillance getting out of hand. Wyndham Lewis, back to the wall in a café, would have said I told you so.

But Nobby was leaning forward over the table, eyes narrowed to points like gimlets at me, plate empty at my expense.

'Is there anything *more* you'd like to tell me, Tim?'

21

When I got back to the bank, I found Penny in a state of great agitation, hopping about outside my office with a creased expression, like a schoolgirl facing an inexorable, uninterruptible forty-minute lesson in religious instruction whilst urgently needing to go to the lavatory.

'Thank heavens you're back,' she blurted out. 'Not too late, either. Jeremy wants you urgently at a meeting. Piers Hargreaves is here unexpectedly. You've to go in straight away.'

'Mustn't keep the great man waiting, eh?'

'No, Tim. You mustn't.'

Her face was perfectly serious. I tried to speculate for a moment on what the grapevine might have told her but decided my first reactions to Hargreaves would be the most dependable ones and obediently sauntered down the passage.

'Ah, Tim.' The two of them were alone, Jeremy behind his desk, looking preoccupied, with Hargreaves sitting cross-legged in front of him. 'I'm glad you were available immediately. Piers has come in for a very confidential chat about the Art Fund and I insisted that you must be present.'

A strand of his long blond hair had come slightly unstuck and hung over one eye, so that he kept pushing it back as he spoke. I suppressed my instant hackle of anger that the pushy outsider should come into Gracechurch Street to interfere with an activity that wasn't his business, then decided I wouldn't snap at Jeremy in what was clearly a harassed moment, probably due to his anticipation of my reaction to something about to be revealed. Public harmony was essential.

Hargreaves, on the other hand, looked impeccable whilst reclining at his ease. He was in dark suit and white shirt with sober tie again, in his estate-agent mode, and I wondered which variations in dress corresponded with which activity he got up to.

'Tim!' He stood up to shake hands with me as I entered and smiled the wide, rather cruel smile I'd seen before. At close quarters, in the sober atmosphere of Jeremy's office, he gave out an even stronger aura of power, of leverage and influence. His eyes seemed more magnetic, more intense than at Bond Street or at his party, and in the more confined space they focused on me with what gave the impression of concentrated curiosity. It was as though a specimen had been presented to him and he was examining it speculatively, with a view to dissection. 'I gather you're well on the way with things at Northampton?'

'Yes.' I shook hands with him and we both sat down. 'I have some facts to check at Companies House, then I'll be just about done.'

'Excellent.' He smiled, the broad shark's smile displaying very bright teeth. 'I knew we could depend on you. It'll be great to get our own printing facilities. Control of the media is essential in a high-profile case like ours.'

'Mmm.'

'You don't agree?'

'If you want to travel from London to New York, you don't necessarily have to buy an airline.'

The smile faded. 'The pre-eminence of the major names in our field has been created by media awareness. We must be certain that we have the resources to sustain our level of exposure. I'll await your report with great interest; I hope you'll appreciate this aspect.' The face had gone stiff. 'Your analogy is both timely and apposite; I have been in the States, you see, at our New York office, and various other meetings.'

'Oh really?'

'Yes.' The broad spiky teeth were once more revealed. 'I

161

heard that while I was away you went fishing for a Wyndham Lewis and hooked a Jackson Pollock instead?'

I grinned modestly back. 'I'm afraid that's how it worked out.'

He laughed, a regulation sort of laugh, nothing natural, you understand, something more obligatory that implied the acknowledgement of a degree of helpless incompetence on my part whilst indicating that there were other thoughts on his mind. 'I knew Charles's programme would yield dividends. Knew it. Chance spin-offs like that will more than balance his absences from Bond Street. Besides, it's giving the younger chaps a chance to do more public reception work while he's away. Must bring the younger element on. I was in New York when the news came through. Just the sort of thing we'll sell well there; fine art is up by thirty per cent in New York. A virtually unknown Jackson Pollock will cause a tremendous stir. The PR boys loved the story; they'll get the most from it, you can be sure.'

'Very good.'

'So all in all, we're grateful to you for following up Charles's lead.'

'Thanks.'

He sat back and crossed his legs in a form of relaxation without diminishing his attention to me. It was not like being a specimen, I decided; more like an item of prey.

He relaxed the look for just a few seconds to put on the more friendly expression of our first meetings. 'I'm still keen, by the way, if you do eventually find a Wyndham Lewis. You will let me know, won't you?'

'Yes,' I heard myself saying, mechanically, 'of course.'

I was thinking of his bedroom and his cocked-ear expression, the magnetic draw Sue seemed to exercise for him, the blending of Nancy Cunard and Alick Schepeler –

'Thanks. It would be great.'

He looked expectantly at Jeremy, who cleared his throat. 'Tim, to the purpose of our meeting: while Piers was in New York he had some discussions with one or two of the galleries there – public ones, I mean – from contacts from his days at the Sherringham.'

162

'Oh yes?'

'It seems that because of people like Hockney and Francis Bacon and so on, there's quite a following, or at least a renewed interest, in Modern British art. Specialized, of course, not as widespread as the Impressionists, but encouraging.'

'So I've heard.'

'Well.' Jeremy hesitated for a moment. 'Perhaps I'd better let Piers tell his own story?'

'Yes.' The toothed smile returned. 'Thank you, Jeremy. As I said, fine art is up by thirty per cent over there. After six years, confidence seemed to have returned. As a result, I had an approach from a major mid-West gallery who have a substantial bequest of money to use for the acquisition of British art.'

'Very good,' I said.

The penny still hadn't dropped. My first thought was how nice for Christerby's to have all that business at the next of their Modern British sales.

'When I say substantial I am talking of double-digit millions. The bequest is very specific, however. It is for a collection of top work.'

'Oh? It'll take them a bit of time, then.'

Still slow, I was, still not cottoning on.

His eyes gleamed. 'Not if they acquire an existing collection. A brilliantly judged one. When I made the suggestion to them, they got very, very excited.'

No, I thought, he can't really mean what I think he might mean, Jeremy wouldn't – after all that effort together he wouldn't –

'It would mean a substantial profit for the investors. But even more important, a substantial profit for the bank.' Hargreaves's eyes, those gleaming, magnetic, woman-fancying eyes, were intently on mine, now. 'And glorious PR too, of course. A fantastic success story.'

I licked my lips carefully before speaking. Something inside me was suspended, hanging, taking the blood from my face. 'Let me get this quite clear. You are saying that you have suggested to someone in America that they should buy the whole of the White's Art Fund collection?'

'Exactly. It is a remarkable tribute to you and Jeremy that they nearly blew their boilers when I made the suggestion. Yours is an amazing, a superb collection. From people like Whistler and Sargent through to the 1930s. Ready made. They'd snap it up.'

'Sell the Art Fund? In one lump?'

Feeling was returning, blood was coming back into my face. I looked at Jeremy with a mixture of awe and horror. I saw that he saw me clearly, was suspended too, poised on the brink of a precipice we'd been travelling too closely together to see in front of us.

'It's logical. It's the logical outcome of any investment activity, surely? To sell at a substantial profit at the right moment in a rising market?'

'And then what? Start again?'

In saying that, I knew I'd answered my own hopeless question.

'I don't think so. Art is not renewable in the same way as stocks and shares. You could not repeat the exercise for the same period of art in the same time scale. You might try another period, but face it: you have, in many ways, reached a plateau with the Art Fund. You have done the job. This is a tremendous opportunity to realize the investment.'

'And then what?' I repeated.

Hargreaves didn't answer. He looked at Jeremy.

'Tim, it's a unique situation. We must consider it very seriously.' Jeremy's blond strand came loose again, and he shoved it back impatiently. 'What Piers says has great logic. It is conceivable that we might start again and put together another similar collection, but I doubt if now is the time. There are different priorities. The board would be sceptical.'

'Surely' – my voice was much calmer than I was – 'the board should be convinced by the very success of this – this sale, if it happened – that we would be capable of doing it again? Not that I'd want to.'

'Exactly! Exactly! You say it yourself: not that you'd want to. The moment would have passed. The Art Fund, in any case, is a fairly static thing. A fund for investors looking at the longer term. We are in a much more dynamic situation now. Movement is essential. The funds realized would be used differently.'

'How?' My voice had gone harsh.

'For goodness' sake, Tim, we are looking at many different things. You know very well what the situation is like.'

'If confidence in art is returning, as Piers says, then surely we should attract more funds on the basis of that confidence?'

'Tim' – Jeremy had an almost desperate look on his face – 'what you say still doesn't alter the facts of the opportunity we are facing. We would be culpable if we did not consider it positively.'

I saw, in his expression, the depth of his feelings. Jeremy was genuinely torn asunder. The Art Fund was a thing he and I had started together, on his initiative, with his backing and his persuasion at main board level, in the teeth of brutal opposition. The fact that we started it so as to have a bit of fun in addition to its responsibilities was something we kept to ourselves; the principal problem of life is so often boredom and Jeremy was easily bored. In recent months, however, the crises of real life had pushed the Art Fund to the back of our activities and my resuscitation of it, in looking for a Wyndham Lewis, was only an acknowledgement of my relative freedom and Jeremy's thrall to the bank's situation. He was otherwise engaged. We had enormous pleasure from the Art Fund, Jeremy and I, but wisdom says that all good things must come to an end.

On the other hand, Jeremy would be the last person to dispose of the Art Fund in a successful flourish just for the sake of saying to the board: there you are, I told you so.

'May we know who the potential bidder is?' I asked, more to gain time than anything else.

Hargreaves shook his head. 'They insist on remaining absolutely confidential. I made a solemn promise I would not reveal their identity until I had discussed the matter with Jeremy and then gone back to obtain their clearance. A thing like this must be highly secret, as I'm sure you'll appreciate.'

My expression must have gone sardonic as my eyes turned from him to meet Jeremy's. This secrecy would be about only one thing: Hargreaves's brokerage. He would aim to extract the maximum amount of brokerage from his contact. On a multi-million deal he'd want at least six figures in commission; it would be just like him to use his contacts from the trusteeship of the Sherringham to make a nice turn on the side.

'There are,' he said, his voice deep and resonant now, 'other implications, of course. If the bank decided to realize its art interest in this way, with a very substantial profit, it might also be the time to re-examine its role at Christerby's. In the light of the strategy I am hoping to adopt, the strategy of a broader field of activity, there are different options and roles for the bank to play. I'm sure Jeremy and the main board will want to think about these as well as the decision on the Fund. It would mean a very different role for you, too, Tim, but I'm sure you'd respond to that positively.'

The sheer brass neck of the man was unbelievable. My wife, the Art Fund and now, in veiled form, my place on Christerby's board; he threatened all three. If I resisted him over Bergendale Press, my job would come next.

Richard White was right. Hargreaves had to be stopped.

At all costs.

But what on earth was he up to? Selling the Art Fund was one thing; reluctantly, emotionally, I had to accept there was a logic to that, however indigestible personally. But to get White's to sell out from Christerby's? What hidden agenda was there in that? It certainly wouldn't serve the purpose Richard had indicated Hargreaves had in mind: a seat on White's board. There'd be less reason if they were detached from the art world and he ran his conglomerate empire separately. He'd need finance to set that up, though, and if White's provided the finance but didn't participate in the equity –

I was speculating. Without nearly enough information.

'Well.' In spite of his own state of shock Jeremy managed to produce a brisk, businesslike, summarizing tone. 'Clearly, we've got a lot to think about. We are deeply grateful to you, Piers, for this discussion. We'll get back to you as soon as we can.'

Always the gentleman, Jeremy; his use of the plural was reassuring.

'Fine.' Hargreaves stood up. 'I should emphasize, though, that it won't wait too long. The market here is still pretty moribund, so this American opportunity is unique; a one-off.'

'Of course.'

Hargreaves went to the door, turned, raised a finger and stiffened himself upright to declaim:

'Our tri-classed life-engine carries oh far more
Back-to-the-engine fares than those face fore –'

He grinned his wolfish grin again. 'Remember that? I hope you are not back-to-the-engine fares, gentlemen. Face fore, please.'

Jeremy stared at him in bewilderment. I decided I'd better translate.

'It's from Wyndham Lewis's poem, "One Way Song", Jeremy. A reminder about our national weakness: being pre-occupied with the past instead of looking forward.'

Hargreaves grinned even wider. 'I'm glad you've read him as well as looked at his art, Tim. He had a brilliant grasp of the realities. The political realities, too. I await your decision, Jeremy.'

He left. Jeremy and I stared at each other.

'Is that man sane?' he asked.

'The City seems to think so.'

He shook his head wonderingly. 'Coffee?' he asked. 'Or would brandy be more appropriate?'

I shook my head and got up.

'There isn't time, Jeremy. There just isn't time any more. I have got work to do and we both need to think carefully about – about this proposal.'

'Let's sleep on it. We'll talk tomorrow, Tim.'

'OK.'

I turned towards the door but he made a restraining gesture.

'Wait. I rather liked that remark of yours about not buying an airline.' He pressed the buzzer for his secretary. 'I think you'd better have a copy of the St Pierre report.'

22

'Like the villain of a North-country novelette.'

Charles Massenaux's words made me think of Charles himself, now probably holding forth to the collecting enthusiasts of Chester, with a nuance here and wry smile there, the cameras running. There'd been a couple of reviews, both very positive, about Charles's first programme. They particularly liked the exposure of the faulty walnut press chest; they said that was what made for fascinating TV. It also seemed that Charles had been enjoying himself, expanding on the subject of a mad Pre-Raphaelite follower of Rossetti's called Smetham; with this sort of personal-biographical content, the reviews predicted, the series could not help but be a success.

If it hadn't been for Hargreaves . . .

That was the thing about the man. In any normal set of circumstances you'd say how can anyone so blatant, so much a caricature of everything so transparently repellent, prosper? Why would normal, rational people follow his bidding? Put him into a repertory company play and the audience would hiss or produce hoots of derision, depending on their bent. Come on, the critical mind says, in real life such men get nowhere.

Like Maxwell? Like real life? Like all those junk-bond dealers, con men, demagogues, preachers, bigamists and serial killers who, afterwards, everyone says were so obvious? Afterwards it is all so clear. While the act is running, however, while the booming voice booms, the outrageous acts are enacted, the sequence of unskirted sirens is seduced, no one moves to stop the show; the damage spreads afar.

But at the time the source of energy, upsetting, disrupting, tearing apart whilst setting up and causing interactions, is difficult to challenge absolutely, condemn without reserve. There are always side-effects and beneficial ripples for somebody, or the sort of challenges we have to admit are necessary to counter our nostalgic, comfort-seeking era.

Our tri-classed life-express carries oh far more
Back-to-the-engine fares than those face fore –

The backward-facers get short shrift from the Hargreaves type; sometimes the enemy becomes your hidden friend.

I read the St Pierre report feverishly. It wasn't a very big outfit but it was owned by another group registered in the Channel Islands. They were quite substantial. They, in turn, were owned by a Liechtenstein trust which, in turn, appeared to be the property of a bank in Zürich –

Zürich?

– and, almost equally, a shareholding in the name of Lamberville Enterprises of Geneva –

Lamberville?

The telephone rang. Penny said, crossly, 'It's that Mr Harry Macdonald again, the one who won't say who he's from.'

'You can put him on in a moment. Before you do, I've an instruction for you: I want photocopies of the exclusive interview Hargreaves's ex-wife gave to that Sunday paper last year. Get it from our cutting agency. Faxed. Now.'

'I – I beg your pardon?'

'You heard, Penny. I want the full article. All the gory details. No cuts. Now.'

'Tim, really.' Penny sounded quite shocked; hypocrisy is quite advanced in the bank's secretarial network. 'Is this really wise? I mean, the cost goes on the budget for research and Geoffrey's terribly sharp about vetting the items.'

'Do as I say. Get it. Now put Macdonald on.'

There was an offended silence, then the line cleared.

'Mr Simpson?' The voice was flat, unemotional, with little trace of accent. I reanimated a mental picture of him: hardish, youngish, brown hair cut short, blue eyes, prominent ears, tweed sports coat, brown jeans, leather sporting shoes. Scrubbed, fit. A man of action holding himself in check, as if waiting to detonate.

'Yes?'

'I'm sorry it's taken a bit of time to come back to you. We've had a little problem – a few hold-ups with the client. It's taken longer than we thought. Mr Brooks asked me to apologize for his non-appearance last week; I hope you got that message?'

'Yes, thank you. I did.'

'He's very sorry, but a meeting delayed him pretty disastrously and he couldn't get a message through to the Cleveland Arms.'

'These things happen.'

'Are you still satisfied with the drawing you bought?'

'Very much so, thank you.'

'Good. Would you be able to come to view the painting tomorrow or the day after? Near Kettering?'

'Kettering?'

'Yes. The client lives reclusively, in a farmhouse near a village called Old. He's agreed to letting you see the painting tomorrow or the day after. Sorry it's such short notice but he's a bit odd, you know.'

'I see. George Welling managed to do his persuasion pretty well, then?'

'Yeah. When would be convenient?'

I thought quickly. 'Tomorrow will do.'

'Fine. Let me give you directions.'

'Will Mr Brooks be there?'

'Oh yes. He'll be there, no fear.'

'And George Welling, of course?'

There was just a slight hesitation, a ticking silence before he answered. 'No. George won't be there.' No explanation, no amplification, but then: 'He set it up, but he's away. Will you be alone?'

'I may bring colleagues.'

'Colleagues? To see the painting?'

'Yes. For something as important as this, it's usual. He – or she – would be a Lewis expert.'

'Ah. Fair enough. May I have the name?'

'His name is Hargreaves. Hers is Sue Simpson. My wife.'

'I see.' There was a pause, as though he was digesting or considering this with a view to refusal. Then he spoke again, unemotionally. 'Good. Well, let me give you the directions.'

I wrote down the directions to a farmhouse outside Old, which turned out to be a hamlet between Northampton and Kettering.

I didn't say a word to him about the false address to the estate agent in Notting Hill Gate, nor about my knowledge of fat George Welling, swinging from a Blenheim Orange near Wellingborough. That could come tomorrow.

I closed the St Pierre report, got up, went through to Jeremy's office and told him the news. His eyebrows nearly went through the roof.

'What! You're going where? Off on a wild goose chase again?'

'I'm going to tell Hargreaves and propose that we meet there. He's cracked about Lewis. No, not just cracked; psychotic. It's kind of business mixed with pleasure, Jeremy. I've thought carefully about this; I suggest that we fax a list of the Art Fund's assets to him, now, detailing the current valuations. We'll say that we'll consider a suitable offer for the sum total. Suitable, that's my word.'

'Tim –'

'Wait for it. Once we have an offer on the table, a firm, serious, committed offer, we'll consider it. Until we get that, it's all air. If I know anything about American public art galleries, a written offer will take time. No one can accuse us of not behaving like responsible trustees. Of course, we'll say that in addition to the stark asset value we'll want a premium for the time, effort and expertise it's taken to assemble that lot. I imagine Hargreaves will also want a douceur. From both sides, if I know my man. I'll wait to see what he says tomorrow.'

'I – I think he will.'

'Once the offer is a serious matter, you and I can decide. Until we get it, no decision is necessary. Meanwhile, I've read Geoffrey's report on St Pierre. Is the bank in Zürich keen to buy us up?'

'They say so.'

'I hope they've got a lot of money ready.'

'They say they have. The board members who know say that they have, too.'

'They wouldn't mind ensuring that St Pierre's leasing contract at Bergendale doesn't go up in smoke, either, I'll bet.'

'Presumably. But that's not a major consideration; that's petty cash.'

'Not to Hargreaves. Pride, you see.'

'He is a proud man, that's true.'

'Norman pride, I think. Did you know about Lamberville? I was told by Mrs Waters at that party. Eric Waters of Medallion's wife; I think she's one of Hargreaves's cast-offs.'

He frowned. 'I'm afraid I'm not well informed on that. But of the possible paternity of Hargreaves, well, the City has long speculated in that same direction you've mentioned.'

'So that's how he's prospered. With money like that behind him, it wouldn't be surprising.'

'There is no concrete evidence. Just rumour.'

'But you and the board were willing to go along with him? Sir Hamish Lang, too?'

'The City is sometimes a very small place, Tim. You have to get on with your neighbours. Especially if the exchequer is emptying rapidly.' He looked at me levelly. 'I don't have to tell you that I'm dead set against any sell-out to anyone.'

'No, you don't. I never imagined anything else. But with muscle like that behind him, Hargreaves might yet build his ridiculous media and auction empire, *and* get a place in the bank.'

'Nothing has been decided yet. I – I had a call from Uncle Richard last night. He made his feelings very clear. A counter-movement may be launched from France.'

'Chance would be a fine thing, Jeremy. Maucourt Frères are in worse shape than us.'

'That's my feeling too.' His eyes had stayed on mine throughout this entire exchange, but now they dropped to the surface of his desk. 'Tim?'

'What?'

'What will be your reaction if this American offer for the Art Fund turns out to be genuine? And generous?'

'Sell.'

Still looking down, I saw him wince. I stared at him fondly. When it comes to the crunch the cold, entrepreneurial spirit in Jeremy has its weak spots. The Art Fund is one of them. It is possibly the only back-to-the-engine, gazing-at-yesterday activity Jeremy has allowed himself for years.

'You – you'd sell?'

'To a generous, big, profit-making offer? There is no choice, is there?'

'I – I suppose not. I am surprised, though, that – that you –'

'Haven't shown any regrets? I'd hate it, Jeremy. You and I have had more life out of the Art Fund than anything else this bank has brought to us. It would be the end of an era.'

'You seem very dry-eyed about it.' The voice had dropped to a reproachful softness.

I stood up. 'That's because I'm dealing with threats, Jeremy. Dealing with threats. The time for wet eyes comes after the threats are removed.'

'I suppose so.'

'Do I go ahead? With the fax listing the assets?'

He nodded. He didn't actually say any words at all.

23

I phoned Piers Hargreaves at his Bond Street number and got his secretary.

'Very sorry, Mr Simpson, he's in a meeting.'

'I'm afraid you'll have to interrupt. Tell him the answer on the Art Fund is yes and that I've laid on a Wyndham Lewis painting for him. For tomorrow. We can discuss the Fund then.'

There was a gasp before she explained that he couldn't be disturbed and had a very important meeting tomorrow anyway so he couldn't possibly go to look at a painting.

'Just tell him what I've said, please. Art Fund and Wyndham Lewis. Tomorrow. Right now, please.'

She wobbled a bit but the tone of my voice wasn't one that brooked any more prevarication. Very shortly, the great man came on the line.

'Tim? Is that right? You've found a Wyndham Lewis?'

'Yes. And we're prepared to accept an offer for the Fund. A fax is coming through to you with the full current asset list and cost details. If we can meet near Kettering tomorrow, we can deal with both items.'

'That's fantastic! My goodness, you're decisive, you and Jeremy. But Kettering?'

'A farm near a village called Old. At eleven tomorrow morning.'

'Old? But that's not too far from our place at West Haddon! Fantastic! I'll stay up there the night with Ellie and toddle over in the morning. Eleven, you say?'

'Yes. Please don't arrive earlier. The old guy is a bit touchy, apparently. So let me roll up first. I'll be there quarter of an hour before. Sue will be coming, too; I want her view.'

'Even better! Much better! You may depend upon it; I'll cancel my other plans!'

'Let me give you directions.'

I gave him the details and rang off. Penny came in with a sheaf of fax paper in her hand and plonked it on my desk. Her expression was quite worth recording; if her face had had many lines, disapproval would have been etched into every one of them. Her mouth was clamped tight shut. Her eyes regarded me with real censorship.

'Reread the details, have you?'

'Certainly not!'

'Liar.'

She blushed, and I grinned. 'No point in not admitting a weakness, Penny, provided it's only to me.'

'I – I really can't think that you –'

'Need this? Oh yes, I do. Very urgently. That reminds me; you said the other day that a Mrs Waters phoned me. I forgot all about it. Did she leave a number?'

'Yes.'

'May I have it, please?'

She gave it and went out as I wrote it down, more disapproval emanating from her.

The newspaper article was scurrilous stuff. My lips twitched at the image of Hargreaves going through the capers described, but there was, very soon, a scowl on my face. I picked up the phone and dialled.

Mrs Waters – Sarah, that was her name, I now remembered – answered after only one ring. Must have been right by the phone.

'Sarah Waters? Tim Simpson. Sorry I've taken so long to return your call.'

'Tim – oh, Tim Simpson. We met at Piers's party, yes?'

'Yes.'

'I – I'm sorry, I've forgotten what it was that I called you about. Isn't it silly? I'm so scatty these days.'

'Not to do with our conversation about Piers, perhaps? Or the Art Fund?'

'Oh, yes! Clever boy! We were saying, weren't we, how

you were going to take him along on one of your buying jaunts?'

'We were, although I explained that that's very confidential.'

'Of course, of course. It's just that I am frightfully interested in your Fund and was thinking of investing myself, you see. And Piers said how brilliant you are. So I caught a sort of conversational fag-end; you know what parties are like. But I hope I didn't put you off Piers? Eric said afterwards that I was frightfully rude about him. Gave me a terrible telling off.'

'Not at all. Piers has been very friendly to me. As a matter of fact, we are meeting tomorrow.'

'Really? Tomorrow? Oh, well, that's great then. I hope your jaunt is successful.' Her voice dropped. 'Tim, if I'm interested in buying in to the Fund, would it be too much to ask you to explain the details?'

'Not at all. I can send you our brochure.'

'I'd like that, but I'd really like a slightly more personal description if possible. Would you be prepared to do that for me?'

I smiled for the first time that afternoon. It isn't often that I get propositioned these days.

'Of course. I'm a bit tied up at present, but I'll send you the brochure and give you a ring once you've had a chance to look at it. How about that?'

'That seems great. I'll look forward to it.'

'It will be my pleasure.' I paused. 'Oh, I have just one question for you, Sarah.'

'Fire away, Tim.'

'It's about Piers Hargreaves.'

'Oh, yes?'

'It's a bit personal. Did he use a photographer?'

'I'm sorry.'

'It must be quite flattering, in a way, to find he's had a sheaf of pictures taken. In the street, wherever. Professionally done but very observant. As evidence of an obsession.'

'I – I haven't the faintest idea what you're talking about.'

Like hell, I thought, like hell.

'He's doing it to Sue now, you see. His last wife – the actress – said she was very flattered at first, when he showed her the expense he was going to. To get pictures of her. All respectable, of course. But dozens of them; in the street, going to work, everywhere. In her case, going to and coming out of the theatre. An actress found it particularly magnetic. Many women would.'

'This – this is meaningless to me.' The voice had gone to a hoarse whisper.

'Oh. I'm sorry. I must have got the wrong impression. It seems he always picks out the best shots. The flattering ones. Very hard for anyone not to at least look at them. I thought perhaps – you know –'

'What are you suggesting?'

If ever a voice betrayed a speaker, hers now did.

I closed my eyes for a moment. There were images all over the back of my retina. The drawings of Iris Barry, Nancy Cunard and Alick Schepeler. An imaginary Jackson Pollock, dotting and trickling into branch-forms with a body hanging from them. Sarah Waters at that party, saying I'm a secretary too, or something like that, and her hard, bold handsome amateur-actress face. The taut remarks about Hargreaves. Her husband's weak, freckled face. A cast-off? Or a current runner? Or hath hell no fury like?

'I just thought you might be able to advise me.'

'You've made a disgraceful mistake!'

She slammed the phone down.

It promptly rang again.

'Mr Merrick for you.' Penny's voice was still disapproving.

'Put him on.'

'Hello, Tim.' The friendly voice of Jim Merrick came booming down the line in a contrast that took seconds to adjust to. 'How are you?'

'I – I'm well. You?'

'I'm even better than I was when I last spoke to you, Tim.'

'Oh? Why is that?'

'I got that stud wall down, now that the painting's gone. And there was the other one.'

'Other one?'

178

My mind was still racing on the theme of Sarah Waters; there was a communications system somewhere I hadn't yet worked out.

'Sure. My mother forgot. There were two. They used two at that panto; the stage needed cover. She'd forgotten all about the other one. Her memory's not what it was. But then, out of sight is out of mind, ain't it? My father must have put it behind there and forgotten it.'

I brought my focus back from infinity and saw the wall opposite my desk as clear as light while I cleared my mind of Mrs Waters and tried to understand what he'd just said. 'Let – let me get this straight. You mean there was a second big canvas in your barn? Behind the stud wall?'

'That's it.'

'Painted over like the last one?'

'Basically. But it's not got a tree and a house on it. They emulsioned a sort of beanstalk up it. With big yellow flowers.'

'Good God. It's the same size as the other one?'

'No; if anything it's bigger. About nine feet square, I'd say.'

I closed my eyes again. This time the images were different.

'Tim? Is it worth sending to your restorer? On the same basis as before? About our agreement, I mean?'

I opened my eyes.

'Yes,' I said. 'I'll make the necessary arrangements.'

'Good man. I really like dealing with you, Tim. I'll have to find some more of these things, won't I?'

'Jim, please don't bank on this being another Jackson Pollock, will you?'

'Oh, I won't.' He chuckled. 'Sunflowers is Van Gogh, isn't it?'

I laughed and put the phone down. I phoned Robert the restorer. His answer is unprintable; shock affects various people's language very differently.

Then I went home.

Sue met me at the door and we sat on the settee while I told her everything that had happened, everything, including Sarah Waters, which made her both smile and frown, but when I went through all the part about Piers Hargreaves, she didn't.

'I'm not coming,' she said.

'Sue! I need you. Especially for a Wyndham Lewis view.'

'No, you don't. Not yet. You'll have to talk a lot of business with Piers Hargreaves and I won't be able to contain myself when I think about those photographs he must have got his private Swiss photographer to take. It's disgusting. Not illegal, I know, not quite, but disgusting. Besides, I'll be superfluous, especially when it comes to this Art Fund offer. Aren't you and Jeremy dreadfully upset?'

I looked at my hands. 'We should have thought further ahead. It never occurred to us that it might all go in one lump. We always saw it as an ongoing process of improvement; disposing and buying, piece by piece.'

'It may come to nothing, Tim.'

'It may. But what about you looking at the Wyndham Lewis tomorrow?'

'You can deal with the painting; you've lots of experience. Authentication can come later. But that's not the reason I don't want to go. I'd love to, normally. You said the other day that you nearly resigned because you didn't want me to be exposed to him. Now you do. What's changed?'

'I can deal with Piers Hargreaves. In fact, I want to deal with Piers Hargreaves. Confront him. Having you there will help, especially if he starts to behave the way he did before.'

'Tim, there must be no violence, you know.'

'Good heavens, I'm much too elderly for that sort of solution to anything, these days.'

She smiled. 'No, you're not. Not at all. Some things about you never change. Although you're learning, fast. I've bought you a present, by the way. It may help.'

'Me? A present?'

She smiled again, got up, went to the bookcase and brought over a big book. When she handed it to me I saw it was Walter Michel's work on Wyndham Lewis, in fine condition, with its glossy wrapper pristine. There, on the cover, Froanna Wyndham Lewis of the *Red Portrait* of 1937 looked pensively towards the titles in a rusty-brown study, cigarette in hand, under the moonlight painting on her mantelpiece and beside her thirties lampshade.

180

'Sue! This must have cost you a bomb!'

I gave her a big kiss and she lowered her eyes modestly. 'You see, I don't always try to dissuade you from what you're after. You'll be much better qualified once you've read that.'

'You are my heart's delight.'

She got up and went into the kitchenette to do something about supper. Out of sheer curiosity I went through the book, exclaiming with pleasure, to the point where Michel catalogues the details of the missing *Kermesse*, sold at Quinn's sale in 1927 for fifteen dollars and advertised maliciously by Dick Wyndham for twenty pounds.

'Good God!' I said, out loud.

Everywhere else I'd read about *Kermesse*, it was described as being nine feet by seven in dimensions. But the description in Michel was meticulously set out: eight feet nine inches by eight feet eleven inches.

Just what a farmer would describe as about nine feet square.

24

At breakfast I tried to persuade Sue to change her mind, but she wouldn't. She was positive, she was cheerful, but she said she knew only too well that this was something I had to fix. You could say that she was playing the woman's card brilliantly, but I don't think in that divisive, resentful sort of way. I kissed her warmly and sallied forth into the grey November morning, getting out into Onslow Gardens to find the car with good time to spare for the journey. I drove out of London to the west this time, instead of threading through crowded streets towards Maida Vale, along the Cromwell Road extension and the M4 to head past Heathrow and join the M25 peripheral motorway, turning north to get round to the M1 at St Albans.

That was where the trouble started.

There was a minor hold-up going out to Heathrow which took me ten minutes or more's patient wait to resolve, but I'd expected that. In a way, it was a good thing because it gave me time to think a bit more about the unsolved line of communication that bothered me and, as I approached the next hold-up, just after the M4–M25 junction, with commuter traffic in a dense volume turning everything down to a crawl, I took up my mobile phone and dialled the number Charles had given me, assuming he was in Chester and that since it was now after nine, he'd be conscious.

He was. 'Tim!' he chortled. 'How are you, dear boy? Not another Jackson Pollock, is there? Or have you moved on to Rothko now?'

'Very funny, Charles. How is the hated performance? The last resort of the respectable, the first of the fictitious?'

He had the decency to sound chastened. 'Rather good, as a matter of fact, Tim. It's going down awfully well with the critics. They say it's the thinking-man's road show. Last night went like a breeze. Two Millais drawings and a super Wilson Steer of Hammersmith, as usual. I really enjoyed it.'

'Well done. Tell me: is Mike Watson anywhere near you?'

'Right here beside me, dear boy.'

'Can you put him on?'

'With pleasure.'

There was a pause, during which the car was able to move about forty yards. I began to feel uneasy. The traffic was starting to get worse.

'Tim?'

'Mike. How are you?'

'Fine, but busy. Charles is an absolute star. What can I do for you?'

'I wanted to ask you about Eric Waters.'

'Oh yes?'

His voice changed inflection, as though I had said something significant.

'What does he do at your company?'

'What did he do, you mean? Not very much, actually.'

'Did? You mean – he's not there any more?'

'Indeed not. Got the bullet about three days ago. I'm not surprised. I don't know how he got the job in the first place. Something to do with Hargreaves, I believe. Anyway, it didn't help him much. He was way out of his depth. There's been another *putsch* and he went out in a night of the long knives. You know what these media companies are like; as bad as publishers. I stay as far clear of head office as I can.'

'Good God.'

'Why, what's up?'

'Nothing. Look, thanks. The traffic's clearing. Got to rush.'

'Me too. Don't forget that beer sometime, Tim.'

'Sure.'

The traffic had suddenly started to move along. I stepped on the accelerator as the signs for Watford and the M1 came up. I would be on schedule after all, but only just. My mind was teeming with the news that Mike Watson had just conveyed, going off on a line of logic like a rocket in tune with the Jaguar as I got the needle into three figures.

As long as Hargreaves was having it off with Sarah Waters, her husband's career was safe, even though he'd been moved from Bergendale's because, presumably, he wasn't up to scratch. Once the obliging Sarah wasn't needed or wasn't obliging any more, especially with a new marriage in hand . . .

Lights flashed up ahead. The traffic stopped again, short of Northampton.

This time it looked worse. Now I remembered the cones they were putting out as I'd driven down the last time and cursed myself for not taking them into account. Nothing was moving at all. I dialled Hargreaves's office and got his secretary, swearing at the lengthy pace the receptionist used to put me through. It seemed to take ages.

'I'm sorry, Mr Simpson' – the secretary sounded triumphant, not having enjoyed my last peremptory call – 'but Mr Hargreaves is unobtainable. He's going to a private meeting.'

'I know that! The meeting is with me, remember? What's his mobile number?'

'He's not available. He particularly didn't wish to be disturbed this morning. He's left the mobile at home and will pick it up later.'

'What? Why did he do that?'

'To obtain privacy, Mr Simpson. All sorts of people call him on his mobile. I can take any messages, of course, and this afternoon he'll – '

I cut her off. The car was stationary, locked into the traffic. You damn fool, I thought, you damn, damn fool.

Nothing was moving, nothing. There must have been an accident as well as the cones. After a fuming while – minutes were ticking past – I wrenched the wheel over and, with hooting and shouting carrying after me, with all my lights flashing, shoved my way across the slow lanes on to the hard shoulder. Then, illegally, dangerously and furiously, expecting a police siren at any moment, I drove up the hard shoulder to junction nineteen, past the serried queues of overheated vehicles and people to get off the motorway and

184

head round Northampton out on to the Market Harborough road, my best route to Old.

It seemed to take an age.

The farmhouse was where Macdonald had said it would be, on a track leading back towards Pitsford Reservoir, another watery view in another watery landscape that made me think of George Welling and had my heart pounding as I sprayed gravel and mud from the Jag's wheels, bumping hard along the rough surface regardless of suspension and anything spiked and agricultural that might suddenly come round the next corner, but nothing did.

The stone farmhouse was grave and silent, its blank windows hung with dirty curtains that might have been those of a neglectful old man or those of a house long abandoned. Hargreaves's Land Rover Discovery was already in the muddy yard, empty. To my right stretched a long, low stone farm building with a pigeon perched on the roof. To my left, what looked like pigsties. They too were empty. A soft, grey, dirty drizzle was falling; rooks cawed hoarsely in some trees across a field.

The countryside at its most dismal and threatening; prickles started down my spine again.

I was just ten minutes late.

Beyond Hargreaves's vehicle stood a dull red Vauxhall Cavalier, J reg, splashed with mud. As I got out of my car and looked at it I heard, from what seemed like inside the house, a cry or call, not that of someone alarmed particularly, but disturbing, not quite fear, not quite one designed to call attention to the crier. Detached, almost.

I strode across the yard to the front door, which had a large iron handle, and went straight in without knocking. I found myself in a large hall with a stone floor, unfurnished. A damp chill struck my clothes and face, the chill of a house long unheated. It might have been an old man's house-chill; a lot of them are like that. It might not. I wanted to believe that was what it was.

Beyond the hall was a passage which I assumed led to kitchens. Doors to my left and right gave access to the front rooms. In front of me was a cold fireplace and beside that, a wide staircase went up to the first floor.

From upstairs just above me I heard a scuffle and another cry, this time a long moaning sound like someone in serious pain.

I went up the staircase two at a time, swerved round the newel post on the landing and, seeing the front bedroom door open and the windows beyond, shot through it into a large room with big sash windows that overlooked the yard.

The door slammed behind me.

I was round on my feet in a quick wheel to see who had slammed it, looking straight into the eye of Harry Macdonald, his back to the door. He braced himself against it, the staring eyes in his shaven head fixed hard on mine. In his hand he held a big knife with a blade about seven inches long, the sort that outdoor shops with camping equipment and guns sell to so-called outdoorsmen to do their nameless filleting with.

It was dripping with blood.

Another moan came to my ears.

The room was furnished half as a bedroom, but there was a sofa and two armchairs in it, like the bedsitting room of an old person who doesn't want to leave it much. Beside the bed there was a table and a bentwood chair.

Sitting in one of the armchairs, groaning, was Mr Brooks. He wasn't neat and tidy, like Ratty in the *Wind in the Willows*, any more. He was slumped over forwards, holding his chest or maybe upper stomach tightly, wrinkling his neat clothes into a blood-soaked bunch against his body. Blood had trickled over his clasping hands. His eyes stared out of his blue-white face at the floor, not seeing me particularly, and his legs twitched each time he moaned. His small, precise mouth was distorted and slack, sagging open to suck in air. My nostrils caught a horrible smell and then I saw, beside the chair, what looked like a pool of vomit, then worse.

On the floor, on a very dirty carpet at the end of a double bed with only a ticking mattress and brown-stained pillows on it, in a curved, closed posture, lay Piers Hargreaves. His grey-suited body looked huge. Blood had soaked into the carpet and then run from its frayed edges out on to the bare unpolished boards of the old, grimy floor into a large pool on the uneven surface. His hands were across his stomach too, where blood had flowed copiously over his expensive shirt and clothes, but that wasn't the most horrifying thing about the sight of Piers Hargreaves.

His throat had been cut.

Only one side of his face was visible to me; the eye was open, glazed with mucous, and his mouth sagged, the lips drawn back to reveal big bright teeth. He was warm, I could guess, but he wasn't breathing; I got another waft of warm, sickly blood-smell, half-sweet, half-savoury.

Mr Brooks let out another moan, a rather weaker one this time.

I looked up from Hargreaves to Macdonald. 'He'll die if he doesn't get attention soon,' I said.

He nodded, almost vaguely, keeping watch in stiff attention. 'Yes,' he said.

'Why him? Mr Brooks? I thought he was on your side.'

'He tried to stop me. He threw up. No guts.'

'Like the other two? Smith and Welling?'

He never took his eyes off me. His ears seemed to stick out even further than they had in Notting Hill. 'I said once I'd stuck Hargreaves I'd cut his throat. I said it.' His voice hardened. 'Pig. Pigs always get their throats cut, you know that?'

He was about seven feet away. The knife was clenched in his right hand, pointed at me. Both knife and hand were mottled with blood, some bright red and some darker, duller, the colour of his Cavalier car. Yet again my nostrils instinctively contracted at the vomit stench, the warm clogging smell of blood. Something closed inside my throat.

Macdonald pushed himself away from the slammed door behind him and stood upright.

'Smith was at the printer's in Leicester,' I said. 'Welling at Bergendale's.' I nodded towards the chalk, staring face of the speechless Mr Brooks. 'I suppose he was at Wappinger's?'

'Yes.'

'You?'

187

Macdonald bared his teeth. 'I was at Medallion.'

Shock went through me. Of course; now it all fitted. Too late.

'You were a cameraman?'

He checked what I'd seen as a slight forward movement. 'How did you guess, Mr Clever Banker?'

'It fits. Redundant?'

'Of course. Thanks to him' – he gestured at the body on the floor – 'and people like you.'

He moved forward again. I should have pleaded with him, perhaps. I should have said no, not me, not people like me, Piers Hargreaves, yes, or try a name like Sir Hamish Lang, or one of those, not me. But it would have been useless; I was his target regardless, now.

'Sarah Waters,' I said.

He stopped again. And then I knew the rest; he'd been the cameraman until he was dropped. He'd taken the snaps of Sarah Waters that Hargreaves ordered before he went in for his seduction, the sort of snaps Hargreaves was using a Swiss for now –

No, he wasn't; Hargreaves would never use a cameraman again. But Sarah Waters was the link, the one to confirm that the Wyndham Lewis-mad Hargreaves was definitely coming, the trap had worked like a charm, I'd be there first –

I'd be there first. I was meant to go first. After all, my bank was as much to blame, in their eyes, as anyone in the City. They meant me to go first.

The only problem was the others didn't have Macdonald's hate in them, not nearly as strongly. They'd bunched together in mutual despair and rage, but only Macdonald had the real guts. He'd used them for as long as he needed. Until now.

'Your name's not really Macdonald,' I said. 'Is it?'

He grinned. 'Turner,' he said. 'Harry Turner.'

Then he jumped.

The knife came swinging in on my left in a flashing arc towards the stomach, as I'd anticipated. I swung away sideways to my left in unison and turned him, so that he was propelled past me and the swing missed, but he was much

188

quicker and stronger than I'd thought. He checked his missing swing and was back on his toes to take another stab before I could either grapple him or get a blow in at him; I had to jump away quickly to avoid the next skewering stab.

Two quick jumps got me to the bedside chair. A bentwood job in ramshackle condition – as I swung it up in my right hand, I heard the hooped back creak – but just the job for lion tamers and anyone else mad enough to think they can repel a killer, provided they've got a ten-foot whip in their other hand, which I hadn't.

He came in regardless, like a bull at the charge.

I heard the front legs crack against his chest as the hooped back of the chair, now in a horizontal position, snapped off in my hand. The knife was coming up and under the pressed seat but my left grabbed his right and stopped it despite the slippery blood and the speed and the force. Terror lends you great strength if you can keep your head. We collided like stags in rut. Bits of chair splintered to the floor.

For a moment we were stationary, clamped together, his face close to mine, red and shaven and staring.

I head-butted him.

It was like butting an iron lamp-post. Stars danced before my eyes and it took several seconds for my vision to clear. It didn't do him any good either, though. He gave out a short gulp or grunt and stopped for a second more than me, giving me a chance to knee him in the groin.

He brought his left round in a windmill swing – I was still holding the right tightly clamped with the knife in it – but windmill swings are useless. With my untrammelled right I had a choice: I could jab him in the ribs, hit him somewhere about the head or grab his throat.

He was much too strong for any of those. I poked him straight in the left eye with my right forefinger, hard.

He let out a piercing scream. The shock of a real eye-jab is too horrible to describe. I remember a match at Blackheath once when a full-back put his thumb deep into my eye when he was handing me off. It wasn't deliberate, just a mistake in the heat of the action, but it felt as though the whole of the soft, sensitive inner squashiness was being scraped out

189

like a snail from a shell. I had to be taken off and the eye was blind for three days.

Macdonald, or rather Turner, stopped his windmill swing in mid-arc and clamped the hand over his eye. The scream died to a bubbling, slobbering noise. I stepped back, letting go of the knife-hand, and hit him, really hard, in the throat. He made one defensive gesture with the knife, stabbing it in my direction, but he was way off and I rammed him against the bedroom wall.

I was all over him then.

He was tough, I'll say that; I hit him so many times – and kicked him – I thought he'd never crack. But my blood was up and I was savage, battle-crazy, mad, for a moment gone beyond recall. Left, right, left, hook, jab, straight left; it took them all to get him down. The knife rattled to the floor and the noise of it stopped me. I stepped back, panting; he slid to the floor. I kicked the knife away.

Brooks had stopped making any noise at all.

I ran down to my car, breathless, sweating, bloody, and there, out in the wet, cold, miserable Midlands countryside, starting phoning like mad.

25

Everyone thinks I did it deliberately. They haven't said so, but I'm sure that's what they think. It started with the police and the ambulance arriving on site. In no time the place was congested with people, all of them officious and brisk, expressing horror but, at the same time, active, stimulated, excited. Quite a few of them knew who Piers Hargreaves was and a local journalist appeared pretty quick smart. I told the police how I was delayed; I explained how I specifically told Hargreaves not to get there before me. But he did; he arrived early anyway, anxious to pip me at the post. That was typical of Hargreaves, I tried to explain that, but they were very suspicious and I'm still not sure that they believed me.

I'm not sure that I care.

Pretty soon they made the connection with George Welling and they called Nobby Roberts while they had me carefully shut into an interview room – we left the farm after what seemed like an age – and Nobby asked to join the investigation right away, to which they agreed.

I did know. When Turner-Macdonald, or Macdonald-Turner, avoided my question about George Welling on the phone, I did know. And as if the prospect of a Wyndham Lewis wasn't enough for Hargreaves, I told him that Sue was coming.

Well, I did ask her.

But I didn't tell them any of that.

Maybe it was subconscious, maybe it wasn't, but I did have a feeling, too, when I phoned Sarah Waters, that the information wouldn't stop there.

I didn't tell anyone that, either.

Nobby came up very quickly and there was a lot of confabulation outside my interview room after the hours had gone by, the local inspector coming in and going out, before Nobby finally came in and sat down in front of me with a long-jawed, wary look that said not again, not again, how can you keep doing this to me? I could tell that he didn't care much for Piers Hargreaves but in the back of his mind he knew too much, too much about me and Sue and what I'd told him. Nobby is so moral and so conscientious that he'd have been troubled if he had a shred of evidence, but he'd been through chapter and verse with the local rozzers and he knew that there wasn't any. All the same, after a while, when to his relief he was convinced, I caught him looking at me with a half-fearful, half-amused expression, wondering. I know he thinks I'm perfectly capable.

Mr Brooks died on the way to hospital. The knife slash to the stomach severed something vital. As it would have with me and as it did to Hargreaves. Eventually they said that Hargreaves was already a goner before Turner cut his throat, although he may still have been alive when his jugular was severed. No one knows what Turner said to Hargreaves before he killed him; he won't answer questions about that. He just grins, or rather he just bares his teeth, according to Nobby. The whole plan was put together to make sure Hargreaves knew, before it happened, why he was to be butchered. A simple killing would have been too easy. The original, demented, ruined four wanted him to know. Very cold-blooded, it was, in theory; there was to be no forgiveness. In practice, three of them fell victim to being human.

The police checked and found that Turner had been chucked out of Medallion TV eighteen months ago, when there was an efficiency drive masterminded by Hargreaves. Turner had been festering over it ever since. He worked as a freelance for a while, particularly in the printing industry, to companies such as Bergendale and Wappinger's and the Leicester firm, which led him to assemble the odd collection of fellow discontents, victims of Hargreaves's attentions, I met in Notting Hill. Everything else I worked out was true.

Eventually they let me go and Nobby offered to drive me home but I said I was OK and got into the Jaguar to tool back gently, not on the M1 but turning off at Northampton to cruise down Watling Street, the A5, past Potterspury and Paulerspury and the turn to the Merricks' farm, thinking and getting my mind back together again, deciding how I was going to break it to Sue.

It wasn't easy. I recounted the whole thing exactly as it happened, fact by fact, dry and unemotional as her eyes widened and little, high, horrified noises came out of her. I poured us both a very stiff drink and let her take it in, her stare fixed on me the whole time.

She hasn't said anything about it being deliberate but from time to time I think she isn't so sure. I catch her looking at me speculatively, out of the corner of her eye. There are other things on her mind now, life moves on, and she's accepted everything I've told her but I still get that look. The strange thing is that it's not altogether disapproving.

The day after it all happened I went into the bank and sat in front of Jeremy's desk as I so often have before and he stared at me for a full thirty seconds without speaking.

'Sir Hamish phoned me last night,' he said, eventually.

'Did he? I can imagine what he must be thinking. He'll have to go through all of his selection process, all over again, with me present this time. I've told Richard, by the way.'

Jeremy nodded vaguely. I didn't tell him that his uncle Richard expressed satisfaction. Tactfully, of course, but satisfaction. The whole of France was on strike because of the government's proposed austerity measures and the Maucourt Frères alternative had turned out to be a dead loss, as I thought it would. Sir Richard White congratulated me but I'm not sure what for; the problems at the bank hadn't gone away.

'St Pierre Investments phoned me this morning,' Jeremy said. 'They made it pretty clear that Lamberville Investments have withdrawn their support.'

'That was quick.'

'It means the whole deal is off.'

'Can't say I'm upset. To have been put into Lamberville's

pocket, and hence that of Piers Hargreaves, wouldn't have been my idea of a happy outcome. I'm glad we're still independent.'

He stared at me. At that moment I realized that he was thinking that I'd fixed it all deliberately. He wasn't going to ask; it will be weeks, maybe months, before Jeremy asks, and then it will be at the end of a long unbuttoned lunch when we're thoroughly relaxed, but one day he will ask. I'll have to be ready with an answer by then.

'We don't know whether there really was an offer for the Art Fund,' he murmured.

'No, we don't. We'll just have to wait. It might have been just an idea Hargreaves put up so he could punt it around his American contacts to make a fat commission. If there has been an approach from a Mid-West gallery or museum, and if Hargreaves really had undertaken to talk to us on their behalf, we'll hear from them in due course. We just have to wait.'

'It's like a Sword of Damocles,' he said, gloomily. 'It may not happen but somehow the Art Fund will never be the same again.'

'That's what happens when you take Piers Hargreaves on board.'

He looked at me with a flash of anger for just a moment. Maybe the reproach was unfair; maybe I was just getting back for the way they neglected me right at the start; the point was that it was true. I said earlier that people can take only so much reality. Hargreaves and Wyndham Lewis were men who should have realized that.

'Are you required by the police any more?'

Jeremy was countering, just to put me back in my place. I sat back and shook my head. 'They've charged Turner with the murder of Brooks and Hargreaves. They don't know about Welling and Smith; Turner denies them and they would be difficult to prove so the police are sticking to the two they know they can bring to a result. Oh, Brooks's name wasn't Brooks, either, Jeremy; it was Bradshaw. I don't know quite why two of the gang took on false names and two didn't; probably because I'd have been the only one to have

194

seen them and I wasn't intended to survive. I have a feeling that the false-name ones were the real plotters and the other two were just hopeless hangers-on. Four redundant men are not the best basis for a murder plot; just a desperate one. Perhaps the reason why Brooks-Bradshaw sent me that newspaper cutting about Smith's death was to assure me of bona fides that didn't exist, to make the point that these were real names without giving himself and Turner away. I'll never know.'

'Dreadful. Appalling. Talk about inheriting the wind. You've had a lucky escape, Tim. Perhaps more of us have.'

I shrugged. 'I don't know about that. They must have quarrelled between themselves quite a lot, about timing and what to do and how to do it. That was the reason for the strange delays. Brooks-Bradshaw started out as the leader and organizer – he was a director at Wappinger's, you know – and he thought he could keep the whole thing closely controlled, like a business organization. Neat, precise, brisk. He hired the flat in Notting Hill, along with the woman to serve tea or coffee if it was needed, thinking it would all be over within the week. Poor Mr Brooks, as I still think of him, with his sense of macabre humour about the Pall Mall Depository; he must have thought you can plan crime more successfully than a business matter, with all its variables and people problems. It wasn't until what they were going to achieve really dawned, and who would actually wield the knife, that the cracks opened up. Smith must have been the first to panic; then Welling's hesitations caused Brooks's non-appearance at the Cleveland Arms.'

'You never told us anything about any of this, Tim.' Jeremy shook his head reproachfully. 'You live a clandestine life in many ways. You can't complain about Wyndham Lewis, you know.'

'There wasn't any Wyndham Lewis painting, Jeremy. That was just bait. They all knew how intensely Hargreaves was a fan, not just of the painting but of some of the philosophical ideas. *Time and Western Man*, those works. It came over loud and clear to anyone who worked with him. They believed correctly that if the lead came through me, he'd be bound to snap at it; they reckoned he'd never be suspicious of me.'

Jeremy looked at me without saying a word. His expression was quite enough.

'George Welling provided the drawing of Iris Barry. No one knows where he got it from. It's likely that the original idea for the bait, the thing that would draw Hargreaves to a suitable, quiet spot, came from Welling; an auctioneer knows the obsessions of collectors only too well.'

I thought, as I said this, that Macdonald-Turner would have done much better on his own; he was a different animal to the others, savage and single-minded in his rage. Maybe it just took the knowledge that there were more like him, or at least nearly like him, mad and angry and hurt enough to say they wanted to get revenge on the man and the system they saw as having ruined their lives, to convince him to do it. Right from the start he saw himself as the dedicated avenger of injustice, the righter of wrongs.

When he stands like an ox in the furrow . . .

'Turner's defence will be interesting, when he comes to trial. He hasn't implicated Sarah Waters; perhaps he did more than just taking photos of her for Hargreaves when Our Late Leader was on the seduction trail. Perhaps they teamed up in a more intimate way. The police may have to work on that one. It makes me feel sorry for Eric Waters; there's not much left for him, now.'

'But he never took to murder, Tim.'

'He only got the chop in the last few days, Jeremy. He might have joined the party, too. Don't see him as a knife-wielder, though. The female of the species is by far the more deadly in his case.'

'Ugh. You are a grisly fellow sometimes, Tim.'

'That's true.'

Suddenly he smiled at me. It was as though relief had swept through him. 'I made a bad mistake at the very beginning. Keeping it all to myself while you were away in France. Next time, I'll be sure to get you in on things from the start.'

'Thank you, Jeremy.'

'I know that Charles thinks the same. He phoned me last night, too. He's becoming quite a celebrity. The programme is going great guns. Have you seen it?'

'No, I can't say I have, Jeremy.'

'You should. He's quite a star now.' Vivacity came back into his voice; Jeremy, as I've said, swings from gloom to enthusiasm in a trice. 'Well, we must get on. There's lots to do. Challenges and projects. The game's not over yet. Shall we meet for lunch?'

'That sounds like a good idea, Jeremy.'

'Excellent. I'll get Geoffrey to join us.'

I left him at his desk and smiled as I nearly knocked down Penny, poised wide-eyed in the corridor outside his office.

'Come on, Penny,' I said, still half-thinking of Charles but also that it was only fair to put her out of her misery. 'Come into my office and I'll tell you all about it at last.'

'I'll bring some coffee,' she said, happily, and fled back down the corridor to break the glad news to Jeremy's secretary while I went in to sit down thoughtfully at my desk for a few moments until she came back.

Jeremy was right; the game wasn't all over, yet.

In a way, Charles was the only fly in the ointment. Charles was going to be such a success that he'd be too busy to talk to me much. I guessed that he certainly thought that I did it deliberately. I'll never be able to persuade Charles that I really intended to get to the farm at Old first. Charles has benefited most from the whole thing and I had a feeling he'd be guilt-ridden about that. He needn't be; he had nothing to reproach himself with, now, except perhaps his attitude at the start of things and maybe the change in his personality. As it turned out, if he needed consolation, he would have to admit that I didn't come out altogether empty-handed, either.

That was the irony of the whole affair.

26

'You better come and see this,' Robert the restorer said on the telephone, so I took Sue with me and we went to his workshop in North London, where the Jackson Pollock was lying on its back with two of his girl assistants picking at it, and the other big, nine-foot-square canvas was standing upright propped against a wall because it was too big for an easel. He'd taken the whitewash and the beanstalk and the sunflowers off it, so that its full original surface was completely revealed.

'Good God!' Sue said, out loud.

It wasn't all sort of blue and Cubist, as I'd thought of from my reading, nor brown, as from one of Willie Desmond's catalogue pieces. It was only marginally Cubist, more the English version called Vorticist really, but then I remembered that Walter Michel wrote that Wyndham Lewis repainted it for John Quinn so that it wasn't drab; it was yellow and red and purple, three festive figures interlaced in a whirling dance of some sort.

'*Kermesse,*' Sue said, with awe in her voice.

'It is signed,' Robert the restorer said. 'There's no doubt. Wyndham Lewis. Congratulations, Tim.'

I think the word *kermesse* comes from a folk festival of the Netherlands or thereabouts, picked up by Lewis on his early travels; he was in Haarlem quite a bit. It is said that the Countess of Drogheda called it *Norwegian Dance* in a letter now immured in the records at Cornell, so scholars can argue the toss.

Who knows? From London to New York, back to London and on to a barn near Towcester. Bought for fifteen dollars and then offered for twenty pounds. No one thought it still existed, if this was really it. There are so many of Lewis's Cubist and Vorticist paintings that are missing, we may have been assuming too much. But that was how I was going to put it into the Art Fund, until someone disproved me.

'Fantastic,' I said.

'Amazing.' Sue was even more emphatic. 'Absolutely smashing. What a painting.'

Kermesse was painted in 1913, when Wyndham Lewis was a young whirlwind, decorating Madame Strindberg's London night-club, the Cave of the Golden Calf, before she decamped to America with his paintings. 1913; the year before he published *Blast* but when he was a friend of Pound – who gave Vorticism its name that year – and Eliot, rampaging to visit Joyce in Paris, electrifying the art establishment yet identifying with the harsh and bitter *Timon of Athens* in superbly illustrated geometries.

But this was *Kermesse*: a dance, male and female figures juxtaposed, dynamic, mechanical, vaulted, buttressed; the work of a man who, according to Julian Symons, saw men and women as 'machines moving, their appendages of ears, nose and hands oddly stuck on, their activities from speech and eating to excretion and copulation awkwardly stuttering and comic'. It was like gawping at a reinforced concrete dance design set out by a fanatical Modernist with the energy of a demon.

We spent a long time looking at its enormous surface, walking back and forth to get better perspectives while the assistants picked away at the Jackson Pollock. Even Robert the restorer was impressed and Robert the restorer has seen it all, art-wise. I thought of what Jeremy and Geoffrey would say when I told them and felt a tremendous inner glee. The irony, of course, was that the meeting in Notting Hill had had nothing to do with it, even though Hargreaves, indirectly, was responsible.

That thought sobered me down a bit.

After quite a long time we bade our farewells to Robert the restorer and came out to sit in the car. I was about to start the engine when Sue restrained me.

'Tell me,' she said. 'I've been thinking: didn't you say that Wyndham Lewis's attitude to women was that their only real purpose was procreation? The perpetuation of the species?'

'Well,' I answered, carefully – one was treading on eggshells here – 'Lewis was not very consistent, you know. He changed his views a lot, really, over the years. Punted a lot of conflicting ideas about. I haven't even scratched the surface of his published works but a scholastic industry spends time discussing them. Rather a split personality, in many ways. Didn't help himself, much.'

'But that was the gist of it, wasn't it?'

'Er, well, yes.'

'Dreadful.' She shook her head, gently. 'I could almost excuse him when I see a painting like that.'

'Oh?'

'Yes. In a way, though I resent it, it is nice to think that I would finally have met with the approval of so great an artist.'

'Met with the approval? Of Lewis? You? How's that?'

'You're very slow today, Tim.' Her blue eyes regarded me merrily. 'But perhaps I'm being unfair. The *Kermesse* painting must still loom large in your mind and I wanted to wait until you'd found it before I told you. I wanted you to get this one over with. And after all, I suppose this isn't the way wives normally announce such events.'

I just sat and gaped at her for a bit until what she'd just told me really sunk in.

'Your face is a picture,' she said. She was laughing as she said it.

Then I grabbed her.

When I think back, there was an obvious explanation to her attitude all the time. I just didn't see it. And as I say, I still get that look, occasionally.

But we have other things to think of, now.